Before her death in July 1997, beloved lesbian-feminist author Chris Anne Wolfe published two Amazon adventure novels – *Shadows of Aggar* and *Fires of Aggar*. But these two volumes are only the first half of the four-part Aggar cycle. Chris Anne also published two stand-alone novels – a time-bending romance, *Annabel and I*, and a retelling of Beauty and the Beast, *Roses and Thorns*.

As her publisher and friend, I was honored to inherit the manuscripts of Chris Anne's remaining novels, short stories, poetry and songs. These hand-written volumes include both remaining Aggar books – *Sands of Aggar* and *Oceans of Aggar* – and more than a dozen retold fairy tales, and original fantasy and contemporary novels. In 2012, with help from Rebecca Fitzgerald, Skye Montague, Noel Meredith and readers from all over the world, we launched Amazons Unite, a publishing house dedicated to Chris Anne's work and other stories set on Aggar. Only Amazons Unite has the right to publish Chris Anne's work and we take great pride in that mission.

Find out more about Amazons Unite's efforts to bring Chris Anne's books to the public and how you can help at: www.ChrisAnneWolfe.com

Jennifer DiMarco
Publisher
Amazons Unite

Roses and Thorns

Beauty and the Beast Retold

Chris Anne Wolfe

Amazons Unite, LLC
Port Orchard ✽ Washington

Roses and Thorns: Beauty and the Beast Retold
copyright 2000; 2007; 2013; 2014 by Amazons Unite, LLC
published by Amazons Unite, LLC

ISBN 978-1495253379
First Edition February 2000
Second Edition March 2001
Third Edition September 2003
Fourth Edition April 2004
Fifth Edition August 2007
Sixth Edition January 2013
Seventh Edition January 2014
0 9 8

Cover design by Jennifer DiMarco
Interior roses by Chris Storm
Interior artplates by Chris Anne Wolfe

All rights reserved, including the right to reproduce this book or portions thereof in any form whatsoever, except in the case of short excerpts for use in reviews of the book. For information about film or other subsidiary rights, please contact: mission@chrisannewolfe.com

This is a work of fiction. Names, characters, locations and all other story elements are the product of the author's imagination and are used fictitiously. Any resemblance to actual persons, living or dead, or other elements in real life is purely coincidental.

Amazons Unite, LLC, is a Washington State nonprofit company focused exclusively on the works an worlds of Chris Anne Wolfe. Its mission is to preserve and publish all of Chris Anne's novels, collections and games, and continue the legacy of her ideas.

Amazons Unite, LLC
7419 Ebbert Drive Southeast
Port Orchard, Washington 98367
www.ChrisAnneWolfe.com
360-550-2071 ph/txt

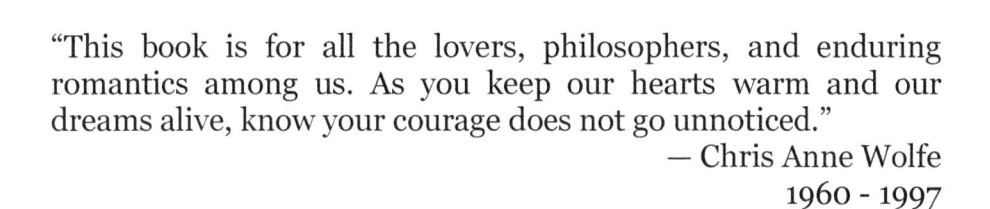

"This book is for all the lovers, philosophers, and enduring romantics among us. As you keep our hearts warm and our dreams alive, know your courage does not go unnoticed."
— Chris Anne Wolfe
1960 - 1997

Roses and Thorns

Beauty and the Beast Retold

Chris Anne Wolfe

Prologue

A woman's hand, strong and lean in its tapering lines, passed over the ripples of the fountain's lowest pool. The words of her spell breathed again, and the splay of dancing waters stilled. Within the calm, a rich garland of black velvet and stars reflected the night of a moonless sky.

"I still see nothing," the man beside her murmured. His remark voiced more puzzlement than concern. "Not even us."

"Patience, Culdun."

The starry images began to swirl. Inky whorls of blackness grew, and a muted crack of thunder loosed.

"There — do you see the forest road?"

Shadows became shapes and took on lighter hues. The figure of a lone horseman appeared. The winds and gathering late-winter storm promised to spare him little on that wooded lane.

"Looks lost enough. He's a merchant of some kind, you said?"

"Aloysius by name."

"Al-o-ish-us." He tongued the odd sounds. But then Culdun found many things strange about these Continent folk. "How did you learn that?"

"What? His name and business?" A dry humor colored the woman's tone. "He mutters to himself."

A weary sigh was Culdun's only response.

"I know. More work for us all, I'm afraid."

"Well," Culdun began grudgingly, "with the storm brewing and wolves prowling, he'd not survive the night unsheltered. If we set the palace wards to ignore him, he should be protected enough against any mumbled follies."

"Aye," the other agreed, even though the mere thought of entertaining any outsider was tiresome. Still, Culdun was correct: this Aloysius wouldn't live to see the dawn without aid.

Her hand swept away the vision of rider and road,

returning the fountain to its gurgling play. She turned hard on a booted heel, voice curt. "Come — we'd best prepare his welcome."

Chapter One

There was no moon that night, not even the merest sliver of one. Clouds crowded above, unseen blankets that smothered whatever bright light the stars would have given, and in the distance thunder stirred. The forest air was chill and damp. Icy tendrils, the claws of viler winds, slipped through the trees to torment the lonesome traveler.

Aloysius shuddered at the baleful cry of a wolf. His horse shied at a twig snapping under hoof. With a curse, the man brought the riding crop down across the animal's withers. The horse tossed his head, squealing, and danced aside, but the merchant had once been a fine horseman.

"It'll take more than a skittering step to unseat me, you brainless old nag!"

With a snorting protest, the horse straightened his step and the merchant rode on.

Aloysius was lost, but he was not about to admit it. If he did, he might begin to believe it. Then he might be tempted to stop for the night and wait for dawn and the sun in order to get his bearings.

The wolf cried. Others answered.

"No, I think not," he muttered, casting a glance behind. The whites of his eyes rolled with the same fear as his horse's now. "A fire and rest? It'd be sheer folly, I think. And this storm, so late in the season —"

Again, the wolves howled.

Thunder shouted suddenly. The horse began to bolt, but a stern tug on the reins broke the impulse in mid-stride. The animal's ears flicked nervously.

Aloysius shivered. The late-winter's daylight was gone now, and the coming storm promised sleet at best and a sudden snow at worst. "I'd almost welcome sleet in this eerie gloom. At least it'd be a tangible sort of thing to suffer."

The horse snorted. The man struck it quiet with his crop.

The wind blew harder, carrying a wailing echo. It was like the mourning cry of a woman — or a dying animal, and Aloysius found himself swallowing hard. He gathered the heavy folds of his cloak around him as his hand strayed to the pistol tucked into his belt. It was loaded with ball and powder, but he was not fool enough to ride with it cocked.

It was rumored that these woods were haunted by magickal, horrible things. That was why he had chosen the route. Ordinarily a man of few superstitions, Aloysius had hoped others' fears would keep him from being followed. He carried relatively little of value from this last trading venture — a single pouch of small, very flawed gems. But he knew at least a dozen pot-bellied fools in the rural regions who would pay far more than they were worth. It would net him a tidy profit, although certainly not a large enough one to squander by engaging a bodyguard. Besides, Aloysius had always held the opinion that guards were not trustworthy. To him, they were a public announcement that the traveler carried money.

He liked to think about the cowards who had periodically betrayed him by abandoning his caravans when finding themselves outnumbered by their assailants. It was not in his nature, however, to ponder the more uncomfortable memories of the times they had not fled.

Still, on a night like this one, Aloysius did rethink the wisdom of his decision to travel alone. Perhaps he should at least have stayed to the main roads and the inns. It was obvious that his shorter route was not proving to be so very short this eve.

Another thunderclap broke. The horse screamed, rearing high, and then everything was suddenly silent. Before the merchant, billows of steamy whiteness shimmered, lifting only slowly. As they dispersed, a shadowy figure was revealed.

The horse froze in place, his hooves planted wide and flat.

There was a *whoosh* of sound and two torches abruptly sprang to life on either side of the stranger, each set high in a brick pillar. The man could now see that he stood before a gate straddling the leaf-strewn road. The wrought iron doors stood open.

Aloysius bent low, clinging to his horse's neck as he peered forward at that cloaked figure. Clad mostly in black, from polished boots to satin shirt and trousers, little else was discernible save the obvious wealth reflected in the quality of those garments. Even the stranger's hands were sheathed in black leather. Both vest and face were hidden beneath the shadows and drape of the blood crimson cloak.

The figure lifted a gloved hand. A breeze circled horse and rider, a warm, scented breeze that teased both Aloysius' cloak and his horse's mane. Then, with a single-finger gesture, the stranger sent the warm wind rushing back through the gates. As it danced up the lane, a string of hanging lanterns appeared, revealing a cobblestone road. The light brightened and Aloysius could now see that the lane was lined with neatly trimmed hedges. The hanging lanterns creaked and swayed in the aftermath of the breeze. Beyond and above the lanterns, spirals of glittering stars, whirling in majestic swirls of light, appeared in the clear, moonless sky. Aloysius was lost in awe.

The merchant straightened in his saddle, barely daring to look around and test his sanity. His horse neighed anxiously, his hoof pawing the ground as the figure stepped to the side of the gate. There was a satisfyingly real clack of boot upon stone with each step.

"No, I am not a ghost." There was humor in the quiet voice.

Aloysius squinted, leaning forward again in an attempt to pierce the dark shadows which hid the cloaked face. As if in defiant response to the merchant's desire, the stranger tossed the cloak's hem over a shoulder, creating deeper shadows. The crimson sheen caught the torchlight, the finely worked velvet and satin caught Aloysius' trained merchant eye, and he momentarily forgot his predicament and fear. But the renewed howling of nearby wolves brought him back to the present moment. Aloysius folded his reins anxiously as he twisted to search the forest behind.

"Now you must choose, Merchant. Me — or them?"

He spun forward, disliking the mocking lilt to that faceless voice.

"You are a demon, not a man!" he shouted rebelliously. He had never heard that sort of light tenor from a mortal male.

The other leaned insolently back against a pillar, arms crossed.

"You laugh at me," Aloysius growled.

"As would you, if you saw yourself looking so hesitant in this dilemma." The low tone of mockery still teased him... dared him. "Come now, is there really a choice?"

Something stirred in the bushes behind Aloysius and he jumped as his horse sidestepped a pace or two.

"Ah," the figure straightened. "Perhaps I have forgotten my manners. I do tend to forget what magic *mortals* fear."

Aloysius did not miss the emphasis in the stranger's choice of words.

"An honorable invitation then? You are chilled, in danger, and — I would also venture to guess — hungry. Good traveler, let me offer you the hospitality of fine wine and warm cheer. Come morning, you may continue on your way. Nothing will be taken from you but a bit of conversation in payment for lodging and good food. You have my word. No, you have my solemn oath." The figure bent in a low, sweeping bow. "What say you, then?"

But the teasing tone that crept into the last question was more infectious this time. The ridiculousness of Aloysius' circumstances dawned on him. With a sudden burst of laughter, the merchant nudged his horse forward.

"Dare I believe you see the jest?" The stranger's head tipped, bemused. "Or is there something comical in my speech?"

"Aye — nay!" Aloysius reined in beside his host, laughing still. "You have the right of it. The jest is indeed on me, good sir —"

"My Liege."

"Pardon?"

"The proper address is not 'sir.' It is 'my Liege.' Go on."

"Yes. Well." His humor reasserted itself quickly. "Of the two, which would any court, my Liege? A wicked end with the wolves, an empty stomach and frostbitten fingers? Or a wicked, magicked end with supper and warm toes?"

A gracious nod and a hand waved him forward.

Aloysius gave a broad, satisfied sigh, pulling the thin stem of the clay pipe from his mouth. For the moment, he was alone in the drawing room as his strange host had been called away to tend to some business.

The merchant took pleasure in finding himself so thoroughly pampered; it had been years since his own merchant's house had flourished. There'd been a few too many bad investments, not enough loyal customers and, eventually, his family had been nearly bankrupt. But, even in his prime, when things had gone exceedingly well, this kind of luxury had been something he had only dreamed about.

His thick fingers caressed the silk embroidery of the ankle-length coat his host had given him to ward off the evening's chill. It was of finer workmanship than he had ever seen, and Aloysius was certain that it had come from the Orient's farthest corners.

His hand moved across the white ruffled silk shirt — also a gift — his fingers delighting in the feel of the fine fabric, and he looked appreciatively again at the woolen breeches and hand-worked vest. The waistcoat, too, was a gorgeous piece of workmanship, with its red satin lining and delicate, exquisite stitching. He sighed. Just the feel of the fabrics reminded him of all that should have been his.

As his business had declined, he had been forced to forgo replacing anything made of silk. Aloysius wondered how he had forgotten the very deliciousness of wearing such proper garments. Drawing on his pipe, he admitted there was little to be done about his circumstances now. The responsibility for that fell to his boys. They would have to do the adventuring. He was growing too old for journeys such as these. And besides, wasn't it about time that his sons began caring for him a little? Yes, he thought. It was. Aloysius turned to bask in the welcoming heat of the hearth as he comfortably assured himself this would be his last journey.

"Sir, your brandy."

The merchant started, shocked to find the servant had come so close without him sensing it. Aloysius, however, was more than surprised when he raised his eyes and met Culdun's steady gaze. He was unnerved. Culdun did not fit his idea of a servant. The man was built as squarely as any burly, hired guard, yet he stood only four feet in height. A small braid hung before his left ear, and the rest of his fine hair, which fell just beyond his collar, was graying.

He did not dress like a servant either. His waistcoat was embroidered in woolen crewel stitch and his shirt was as fine a silk weave as the one Aloysius wore. He wore his collar buttons undone, which was unheard of in any servant Aloysius knew. And if the fact that his burnished brown boots never made a sound when he walked was not enough, the merchant found the blue, green and red tattoos which covered Culdun's forearms indeed confirmed that he was a creature from the netherworld. As the man extended the brandy tray, Aloysius realized that the entwining patterns of vines and snakes were the very same as the ones that were embroidered onto Culdun's waistcoat. Culdun was a most unpleasant reminder that this place was not built entirely for mortals.

"Ah, you do not like brandy then?"

Aloysius jumped, startled again, this time at the sudden appearance of his host. "No," he said quickly, taking one of two glasses on the silver tray. "Brandy after dinner is quite a pleasure."

"Thank you, Culdun."

Aloysius watched as his host, hand still sheathed in fine black leather, took the other brandy.

"You're welcome, my Liege."

Aloysius stirred uncomfortably as the cloaked figure bent in a slight bow. He had never heard of bowing to one's servants.

"Forgive me for my absence." The other straightened, half-turning towards him. "You were telling me of your family at dinner. You sound very proud of your two sons."

"Aye, I am." Aloysius felt his tension ease as the conversation turned to a familiar topic. His shoulders pushed back as he boasted, "The youngest's something of a rake yet. Still into the wine a bit too often. Hasn't grasped a proper sense of responsibility. But that will come. Now my older one —"

"Yes," the faintest touch of mockery resurfaced, "the one that reminds you of yourself in younger years."

"Similar, yes, similar. But more daring, and maybe even more clever. Needs to rein in his temper a tad more, though. Still, that wisdom comes with age, doesn't it?"

"Sometimes."

Aloysius wasn't certain he liked the way that sounded.

"And you mentioned a wife, did you not? Angelique?"

At that the merchant chuckled, again shrugging off his discomfort. "I have a wife, aye, but Angelique is my daughter."

"Ah, forgive me. When you'd mentioned her tending the cooking, I thought —"

"Natural mistake, natural mistake. No, my wife is an invalid, an illness of the bones, you see. She's been bedridden since the birth of our last child. He was... stillborn."

"My condolences."

Aloysius waved his hand. "No need. That's many years past. And I have my boys."

"And your daughter."

"And my daughter. Good lass," he paused and then added with a small smile, "Well, mostly. Only need to take the strap to her now and again. Don't know what I would have done about the household without her. Raised her younger brother more than my wife did. Still, she's got a wee streak of independence that runs away with her once in a while."

"A mind of her own?" the other offered, voice suddenly tight.

"Aye, you could say that at the very least!" He chuckled, not noticing the change. "Mind you, it's nothing a firm handling can't dissuade. Most of the time, you'd never notice it!"

Aloysius blinked in shock and surprise as the brandy glass shattered in his host's black-gloved fist. He stood warily, wondering what had caused such a reaction, wondering if this place was indeed safer than the woods and the wolves. He was even more shocked when his host said, "Tell me, sir. Is she of a marrying age?"

Aloysius dropped his own glass.

His host looked down at the two broken glasses as if seeing the shards and splinters of crystal for the first time. Before Aloysius could voice an apology, his host waved a gloved hand toward the floor and the glistening shards and brandy stains disappeared from the rug and flagstones.

Aloysius groped behind him, knees buckling. The gloved hand moved again. A heavy chair slid forward silently and Aloysius sat with a bump. His eyes were wide with terror.

Quite unperturbed, his host leaned casually against the mantel stone, arms crossed. The cloak's crimson threads shimmered in the dancing firelight, like glinting eyes of watching serpents.

Aloysius shut his mouth with a snap, then cleared his throat and attempted, awkwardly, to settle more securely into his chair.

"If I have insulted you, sir, I can only plead ignorance," his host began. "We are so isolated here. I thought that a merchant of your ambitions would surely have hoped to arrange a... profitable marriage for your daughter?"

Aloysius gaped. A hundred thoughts swirled in his head. After a moment, he swallowed hard before asking, "Am I to understand you are in need of a wife?"

Sarcasm tainted the reply. "So surprising, but true."

"And... and you wish to marry Angelique?"

"Perhaps." The poisonous taint vanished from the voice. "I wish to explore the possibility."

The merchant said nothing. The other continued quite matter-of-factly. "I am in a position to offer you quite a good contract, Aloysius."

"Contract?"

"Is that not the proper term for it? What do you call it then, a bride price?"

Opportunity awakened greed in the pit of Aloysius' stomach. He thought again of the fine garments that now clothed his body and had a momentary vision of retiring into a life of luxury. Licking his lips nervously, he shifted his gaze quickly to the fire. Opposing thoughts warred within him as part of him shouted that this was too preposterous even to contemplate.

"Come now," the host's voice cajoled gently. "It would be a good life for any woman. My father was a Count as was his father and his father before him. My lineage is impeccable. And, as I'm sure you've noticed, I am not poverty stricken."

The merchant nodded slowly. He was intrigued, true, but unconvinced.

"The palace, the village, indeed, the entire valley has prospered by my hand."

The man shuddered. While his host's words were true, he'd heard stories of the surrounding woods his whole life. Many of them were frightening and — given what he'd already seen here tonight — more true than he had imagined.

The other had continued to speak as if unaware of his hesitation. "...And," the voice dropped low, tempting him, "I could offer you much the same. How does this sound: A dozen bolts of undyed silks, another dozen of the finest colors? Tapestries of hand-woven wool dyed with Persian stains? Or perhaps you prefer exquisite jewelry? Crafted silver and gold, gems cut flawless to any eye? Enough to provide for your family's care as well as for your trading house? Or maybe you would like both."

The host paused here and waited for Aloysius to raise his eyes. When their gazes met, the other said, "It would be a contract solely between us. In exchange for your daughter's hand, I will provide shipments every third month. For life. Transport at my expense. She will have an easy life. Rest assured. She will dine every night as you have, wear silks and woolens as fine as yours — be mistress of this palace and all the lands about it."

The faceless figure towered suddenly over him. "Tell me, merchant, does your daughter have a price?"

"Yes."

Mocking laughter rang in the air as his host turned. A glass of brandy appeared on the mantel just as a black-gloved hand reached out. The garbed figure tilted the liquid into the shadow where a face must have been and then replaced the empty glass on the mantle, where it vanished.

"But — but she must agree to it!" Aloysius stuttered, trying to regain some control over a situation spinning quickly from his grasp.

"Oh, yes!" The slow hiss of sarcasm taunted him. "Yes, she *must*. You understand nothing unless you understand that, my dear fellow."

"Why —? I don't follow?"

"Angelique must be told everything, Aloysius. She must be told how this marriage will save your poor, dying house and, more than that, restore it to rich splendor! She must be told about the pampering and benefits this marriage would bring your beloved, crippled wife. Of how it will launch her brothers into the best of circles!

"But!" and here that frightening figure once again rounded on him. "She must also be told of the enchantment."

"She'd never —"

"Oh, yes! She must know this is a magicked place with secrets too ancient to be revealed! She must know she comes to *me*... the most perverted, grotesque of creatures known to this earth!"

Silence descended like a fist. The host's gloved hands gripped the mantelpiece, head bowed and slightly turned away. The stillness lingered, and then was broken by the merchant's hoarse voice, "Shipments every two months."

The other drew in a sharp breath. A terrible tension engulfed the room. And then laughter sprang suddenly from the stranger, wild and almost hysterical, and echoed in the high vaulted ceilings and the corridors beyond.

Abruptly, and before Aloysius could get his answer, Culdun appeared at the man's elbow.

"I will show you to your quarters, sir."

Aloysius rose, shaking, and followed.

"Merchant!"

The man paused in the doorway but did not look back.

"Every two months — until your death. Culdun will see the first lot is ready to go with you in the morning. In two week's time, I will send an escort for your daughter — or for return of the goods."

Aloysius stiffened. Had he really sold his daughter to this... creature?

"And merchant —"

His heart choked his throat in fear. What else would be asked of him?

"Tell her, I will not beat her."

Of everything he expected to hear, this was not among the possibilities. Disbelief muted him.

"You will tell her — *swear it!*"

"By my oath!" he nearly screamed in his anxiety and fear.

"Good." The other turned away and the merchant was led to his rooms.

When Culdun returned, the other was standing in the same place as still as stone.

"My Liege?" Culdun ventured.

"Yes, Culdun?"

"Will you send the token rose as usual?"

For a long moment, no reply. Then the cloaked figure nodded. "Everything as usual, Culdun. I'll leave it up to you."

"Yes, my Liege."

After he departed, the only company in the room was loneliness. The fire crackled as a log settled. A ticking echoed from the tall clock standing in the corner. The midnight hour chimed.

A hand lifted to push the red cloak back and uncover hair of the darkest ebony. Unruly and curly, it fell to shoulder length, poking out of the silver clasp which fastened at the nape. The face was shadowed with grief. The long lines of nose and delicate cheekbones were sharpened, almost gaunt, with a haunting despair. The dark eyes and the slender arch of brow reflected only emptiness.

Head bent, burying a smooth forehead against the still-cloaked crook of an arm, shoulders shuddering, the Liege cried.

Chapter Two

Angelique leaned against the wall, gazing down into the worn, empty courtyard from her window seat. She turned her neck a little, easing the stiffness in her shoulder. Behind her, in the small room, her mother's raspy breathing rose and fell in a familiar rhythm.

He had beaten her again, but had taken to using his bare hands – she would be sore for a while, but the bruises, if any, would be less than those from a strap. After all, his heart hadn't really been in it. Angelique couldn't remember what she had or hadn't done. She knew it really had nothing to do with her chores. Aloysius was upset because she had not agreed to this marriage, although she had not objected either. He had said she had two weeks to decide. It had barely been one.

In her hands, she held the silver rose. It was beautifully crafted, the shimmering light bright white against its polished finish. There were veins etched in its single leaf, and the petals were half-opened. The thorns pricked as sharply as those of any real bud. The thorns. They were unsettling reminders of life's realities. Despite Aloysius' assurances, Angelique hardly knew anything about this noble.

But Angelique knew Aloysius. He was a man who might mean well at one time or another, but his own selfishness often won out over the needs of others. A new pair of boots for his favored eldest, Ivan, would take precedence over coal for Mama's room, since outward appearances reflected well on him. And profit always won out over honesty. There wasn't much that didn't take precedence over his bastard daughter-by-marriage.

Angelique doubted that he had mentioned that little scandalous secret to her prospective suitor. It was something never mentioned outside the family, and she knew it must have been a relief when Aloysius discovered her mother's lover hadn't left some noticeable mark of paternity upon the daughter. Her eyes were the same color as her mother's and her hair the same burnished brown as Ivan's. Of the three of them, only Phillip had Aloysius' lighter coloring.

A droll smile tilted her mouth as Angelique thought of Ivan. Not for the first time did she wonder if perhaps he was her full-blood brother. There was a certain amount of irony in that possibility, given Ivan's favored position. But that was a private speculation that Angelique had never shared. Disgracing Ivan would not change anything; it would only cause pain. So she had kept her suspicions to herself. She was not one given much to vengeance.

Now there could be money enough to reopen the servant's quarters, which also meant more care for Mama. She knew Aloysius was wary of gossip, and he would find a nursemaid or two for his wife merely to ensure that the rest of the city did not accuse him of neglect. After all, such a reputation was not good for business. And finally there would be fuel enough to keep this little room warm, winter and summer both.

"Angelique?"

Her mother's voice called the young woman out of her musings and she went to the bedside quickly, her bare feet making little noise on the barren, wood floor. She smiled, the tenderness she felt for her mother bringing a warm glow to her face, and gently lifted the fragile woman into a sitting position. With practiced swiftness, she plumped up the pillows and re-tucked the tattered quilt.

"Do you have time to talk with me today?"

"I always have time to talk with you," Angelique replied with a smile, as she curled a leg up under her skirts and carefully settled herself on the bed.

"Do you still have the rose?"

"Yes." She reached to the bedside table to retrieve it.

Her mother's trembling hands took the slender sculpture. Her mother had been fascinated by the rose ever since Aloysius' return. Angelique felt no need to warn her of the thorns. She knew well of thorns.

"This noble must be a tender soul."

Curious, Angelique tipped her head, pushing the dark waves of her hair over a shoulder. "Why do you say that,

The Decision

Mama?"

"The detail." Fingers, joints thickened by arthritis, trembled beneath the leaf. "Only a man sensitive to beauty would send this rose. One such as my husband would have sent a less exquisite piece, a piece that was measured by the weight of silver rather than the workmanship. A man like my husband would find the silver more precious than the craft of sculpting it." Carefully, her mother handed the rose back to Angelique. "What has he told you of this man?"

"You know what Aloysius has said, Mama. I've told you a dozen times."

"Tell me again."

It was then Angelique realized how much her mother wanted her to marry this noble. It was not for the family business nor for the luxuries it would bring Mama, but because she wanted to know Angelique would have all those things she could not provide.

"Tell me, Angelique. What did he say?"

"Well, he's said a great many things." Gently, she took her mother's hand. "He says the palace is a magickal place with walls covered in beautiful tapestries and the finest carpets from the Orient covering the floor. He says the woodcraft of table and chair, clocks and railings could not be finer in a German Meister's shop."

"A prosperous house."

"Yes." Angelique smiled at her mother's child-like eagerness. "It is a very prosperous house, Mama. Garments only of the finest spun silk, food prepared with only the best ingredients and with most exquisite care. It is as prosperous as the village and lands beholden to it."

"You would never have want of anything."

"No, never in such a wondrous place."

"And the Liege?"

"Aloysius says the Liege is honorable. One who keeps promises and has brought prosperity to all in the land." Angelique's smile was strained as she remembered there was no specific name, no specific anything attached to this suitor. Aloysius' vagueness in describing the head of this household was legitimately disconcerting. She knew it was likely this noble was balding, pot-bellied and suffering from gout in at least one of his legs.

"But he values people, he said?"

"Yes… yes, he did say that." Angelique pulled herself back from her thoughts with an effort. "He said this Liege was respectful even of his servants – giving them little bows of acknowledgment and so forth."

"A kind man." Her mother patted Angelique's hand. "And he would not beat you."

"He said he would not." Angelique swallowed hard; her mother knew of Aloysius' temper, although they never spoke openly of it.

"Money, position, a home of beauty. So much you could never have here, my love."

Angelique moved nearer, slipping an arm around her mother's shoulders as tears threatened to spill down her cheeks. "But if I left, I would not have you."

Angelique's mother shook her head tiredly. "You will not have me forever, child. And I worry that you will be too old for marrying if you wait for my death."

Angelique's reply was a soft chuckle and a gentle hug. "Then I simply will not marry."

"And when the boys do?"

Angelique shifted uncomfortably. The thought of being the kitchen maid to her brothers' families had never been an appealing idea, but it was a realistic one.

"There are many things that are uncertain in our lives, Angelique." Her mother's eyes began to close. The effort of talking and sitting had begun to take its toll. "It may be that marriage to an old pot-belly would be less terrible than the drafts of the kitchen maid's attic room. But it may be more repulsive to share your bed with someone like that than to scrub the hearthstones. You must decide which you will risk."

"It will be alright, Mama." Angelique fought her own tears as she settled the thin, small woman back under the quilt. Her mother's frailty, her skin so icy cold even on such a warm day, frightened her.

Her gaze fell to the nightstand where the silver rose lay. In spite of Aloysius' half-truths, Angelique knew what her decision would be.

It seemed inevitable.

Chapter Three

Although it was midmorning, the damp mists of dawn still lingered. Aloysius paced the parlor floorboards, muttering about the time and how he really ought to be in town with his sons. It didn't seem right to him to leave his new shop without its proprietor's care so soon.

But when Aloysius had started to mumble about the blessings of a house that skirted the city's edge, Angelique had fled to her mother's room. Her stomach was tied in enough knots without being reminded of his own misgivings. And she knew that he had them, even if he wouldn't voice them directly for fear of discouraging her.

So she had quietly taken her window seat above the courtyard and schooled herself to wait. Her mother's faint snore was reassuring, and Angelique was relieved that the sleeping powder had finally taken effect. She half-wished the woman would awaken, but they had said their good-byes at dawn, and it had been days since her mother had slept well.

Below, boards creaked under Aloysius' feet and she sighed. A breeze fluttered past the tattered lace curtain. The scents of dusty straw and sweaty horses mingled with a green freshness from the meadows beyond. The soft coolness of the woods that lined the road came to her too, and Angelique heard a bird begin a friendly squabble with its neighbor somewhere. Spring was here at last.

She felt vaguely sad at leaving. She had spent her entire life in this house. She knew every worn piece of linen, every unraveled thread in the carpets, every splintered edge of wood. It was a familiar place, and her mother's room had always been welcoming. But this had never been her home. She had never felt she truly belonged here. Aloysius and her brothers hadn't let her forget that she disgraced them, and therefore herself, with her very existence.

Then, suddenly, she had a choice. Since her decision to

leave had been announced, Aloysius and her brothers had begun to treat her differently, almost considerately. The change amused her, but it hadn't made her feel any more a part of their family.

It was strange, but as this day drew closer, Angelique had become aware of a growing excitement that was replacing her initial anxiety. A faint hope formed within her that somehow this new life would welcome her and she would find a place where she could belong. She held onto that hope tenaciously.

The clatter of horse and carriage across the cobblestones broke the quiet. Angelique pulled herself up with a start and peered through the thin lace. Her eyes widened at the sight of six matched grays and the white carriage. Aloysius hurried out to greet the small man who climbed down from his seat beside the driver. Her nerves fluttered as she realized the manservant was declining to enter the house. It was time. She was actually leaving.

Hastily Angelique stood, glancing at her dress and smoothing the blue-gray silk down over the layers of petticoats. She had never worn a dress this fine, although the fashion was simple as she was travelling. Since the journey would be two or three days, she had declined Aloysius' offer of a hoop skirt or tighter corset.

She picked up her heavy shawl. Hand-knitted and embroidered with small flowers along the fringed hem, it was not very fashionable. But it was her shawl, made by her mother years ago, and it was the only thing she was taking that truly belonged to her. Her trousseau was to be a gift from her betrothed, Aloysius had explained. All she needed to bring was the silver rose. She was to present it to the nobleman herself as proof of her promise to marry.

Angelique checked again to be sure the rose was in her drawstring purse. Then she touched a quick hand to her hair; the silver combs seemed secure. The usual tumbling mass of her hair was cooperating for the moment.

She took a deep breath, a slow one since the little-used corset wouldn't allow any other kind. Her eyes fell tenderly on her mother's sleeping figure. She wouldn't risk a kiss but would remember the peaceful smile. It had been a long time since she had seen that special smile on her mother's lips.

Aloysius met her at the foot of the stairs. Angelique indulged him as he hugged her and murmured something about how beautiful she looked. Then he was hustling her through the house to the courtyard.

"Now be tolerant, girl. All servants seem a bit strange at times. Just remember you're the mistress, and everything will come out right."

Angelique looked at him sideways, not quite understanding what he was talking about and musing that he, of anyone, had little or no idea of how servants should be treated. Given her personal experience with his rather absurd expectations, she guessed their opinions were different on how any household should be run.

"Angelique, this is Culdun. He's the palace steward."

"Good day, miss." Culdun bowed politely, and Angelique tipped her head in acknowledgment despite Aloysius' protesting squeeze on her elbow. "Your father says you have accepted the terms of the proposal."

Angelique swallowed hard. "Yes."

Culdun studied her frankly, his dark gray eyes fastened on her face. As Angelique looked back, she got the impression his eyes had seen much and that he was far older than he seemed. And she saw kindness, too. In that first instant, Angelique knew that Culdun was an extraordinary man. Aloysius was right; he was no mere servant. She thought she might like him, even if his little braid and odd-colored eyes seemed strange to her initially.

"I am to ask again." His eyes held her directly. "Do you come of your own free will?"

This time there was more determination in her answer. "Yes, I do."

Culdun appeared satisfied, and Aloysius finally let go of the breath he'd been holding.

The steward stepped back to open the carriage door, the coach steps unfolding at a touch. "If you will, Mistress? Our escort is waiting."

Angelique could see a half-dozen horsemen of Culdun's

size beyond the gate at the road. They were well-armed and sat astride sturdy beasts. The horses that had been tethered beside the barn, which Aloysius had used to bring home the silk and silver that were her bride price, waited there as well.

"Aye, girl, it's farewell," Aloysius said. Angelique submitted to another brief hug. "Be sure to write us now. Your mother'll be pleased for word."

She nodded, pausing to look up at that window. Briskly, Angelique turned. She had said her good-byes.

Culdun offered a hand to steady her climb. He smiled encouragingly as she murmured a thank you, but her sight was blurred with tears and she didn't see it.

Angelique wasn't certain how long they'd been driving, although she was grateful for the time alone. She hadn't expected to cry. It was something she seldom did. But after a bit, her tears stopped, and she became more aware of her surroundings.

It was as grand a carriage as the six matched horses had suggested. Its simple lines outside, however, had given little hint to the extent of luxury within. She sat facing forward on a full bench lined in crushed, red velvet. The seat was thickly padded and slanted back at a comfortable angle so that the larger bumps and potholes did not throw her about too severely. Across from Angelique was a half-bench, similarly cushioned. Beside it stood a cabinet which had deep holes set into its top for decanters. A glass covered tray with fruits and sweetbreads was nestled into the cabinet-top next to a decanter of wine. On the wall beside the cabinet, where a window should have been, leather pockets were neatly arranged to hold glasses and silverware. Small lanterns flanked the doors, delicate pink-glassed chimneys hanging in little brass rings. Directly above them were narrow slits in the roofing which drew the smoke away when they were lit.

But what most took her breath away, however, was the slender vase affixed to the wall beside the door she had entered.

It held a single pink rose, a bud barely in bloom. Angelique lifted it gently from the glass, wary of thorns, only to find someone had carefully stripped it of those sharp barbs. She wondered again about this lonely noble who lived in such isolation.

There was a knock at the door, but, before she could respond, the door opened without the carriage halting and Culdun climbed deftly in. He took the seat opposite her. "I trust that I am not intruding, my Lady?"

"No, not at all."

He nodded in satisfaction, settling himself more comfortably as he tugged down the sleeves of his coat. Angelique noticed the box step that had been built into the floor beneath his seat. It compensated for the man's shorter height, so that his feet could rest there instead of dangling.

"I see you found the rose."

Angelique smiled, again lifting the pale bud to smell the light, sweet scent. "Was this your doing, Culdun?"

His smile was kind as he answered, "I admit I'd been thinking I should, miss. But as it turned out, I found my Liege had already attended to it... just as you were hoping."

She laughed faintly. "Am I so transparent?"

"No, only nervous. It's the least one can expect given the circumstances, isn't it?"

His eyes lost their tenderness, replaced by a searching intensity. Angelique frowned, trying to decipher the unspoken part of his question.

"I'm sorry." He passed a hand tiredly over his face. "I've come to offer you a chance for questions, not make you frown."

"Questions?"

"Aye," he grinned broadly, gray eyes twinkling again. "Such as how long is the journey?"

"I was curious," Angelique admitted cheerfully.

"Well, that depends on you."

"Oh?"

"We've fresh horses posted along the way, and it's quite possible to pull straight through. But traveling is not much fun for the less experienced. My Liege has no wish to exhaust you for the sake of a day or two.

"If we drive through, we'll arrive tomorrow afternoon."

"So soon?"

"Aye, we've a swift lot of horses. However, we've also brought pavilions and comforts for overnights if you'd rather stop for the evenings. In that case, we'd be out for three or three-and-a-half days."

"Sounds like an awful lot of bother for just one person's comfort," Angelique mused.

Culdun chuckled, but assured her, "It would not be a bother, miss. And I do not expect you to answer me now or in the hour. You simply manage as far as you feel capable and then tell us. We'll call a halt for you. If you feel the need to stretch your legs, we can make a stop at any time you'd like. And, of course, you're always welcome to walk about when the horses are being changed."

"That is most kind. But I must say I disagree with you, Culdun," Angelique murmured with a half-smile, eyes on the rose in her hand. "You are taking an awful lot of trouble over me."

His responding laughter was soft and friendly, making Angelique feel less alone than she had for years.

"What else may I ask you, Culdun?"

"What else would you like to know, my Lady?"

She moistened her lips, her mind jumbled with all the things Aloysius had not been able to say. "Can you tell me about...?"

"My Liege?"

Anxiously, she nodded.

"What has your father said?"

"Very little."

"And yet you are here?" Suspicion suddenly separated him from her again.

Angelique's voice was firm. "My reasons are my own, Culdun."

"Mistress," he acknowledged, tipping his head, his growing respect evident. "I did not mean to pry."

She held her silence then, turning to replace the rose

before wrapping her shawl more securely around her. As her gaze drifted to the window and the passing scenery, Culdun waited patiently.

The carriage rattled and swayed over a particularly bad bit of road. Angelique barely seemed to notice, but when they had settled into a smoother ride, she ventured, "Does he have a name, Culdun?"

"A given name? Drew."

"Andrew?" She looked at him finally.

"Drew," Culdun repeated succinctly.

"Aloysius said," her gaze returned to the window, "his – my Liege's father was a count?"

"Parents? Yes, Drew's father was a nobleman. Drew's mother died in childbirth. There was a stepmother. She came in the later years. But for a long time there was only the father and the child. I must admit, I did not know the parents. They did not live at this estate."

Angelique nodded faintly. "There is a village?"

"Yes, it is a small community hidden in the woods beyond the palace grounds. There are common lands for farming. A good forest for hunting, although we do not grant outsiders hunting privileges. Not even for wolves. My Liege is strongly committed to the safety of all within our little valley and that protection extends to the animals of our forests as well as to the people. And since we are self-sufficient, my Liege has never found reason to humor the neighboring poachers. Hunting for sport is simply not allowed."

Angelique raised her eyebrows in response to this bit of information.

"You disapprove of this policy?" Culdun prompted, watching her closely.

"It is..." She hesitated, shaking her head and choosing her words carefully. "It is a different perspective. It seems reasonable."

"But?"

"The villagers do not object?" Her brothers were always speculating about bounties for wolf pelts. She imagined many families could have used such extra money. But if the village prospered, what need would they have for that dangerous sport?

Angelique realized suddenly that Culdun had not answered her. She shifted about, nestling comfortably into the corner, and faced him. His eyes were studying her again. She said nothing to distract him, but rather folded her hands and waited.

Culdun began to nod, and then he murmured, "Your father said you were independent."

Angelique blushed, but admitted, "I have been so accused."

His voice took on a much more assured tone. "I think the man was right. You have a mind of your own." He made it sound like a compliment, and it drew a smile from her. "Will you permit me to show you something?"

At her curious nod, he began to shed his coat. "Our villagers are—" he grinned crookedly, "of a different perspective too. We would each give our life for our Liege. The valley has become a sanctuary for us as well as for the animals.

"Originally my folk came from the deep woods of England and from the Emerald Isles beyond. Centuries ago most of us were forced into exile. It was a bitter time, and I still vividly remember that last battle of my childhood." He rolled back his sleeves and astonishment chased aside the confusion his words had created. Culdun smiled again. He was pleased at the curiosity that made her lean forward as he extended his arms.

"My folk are known simply as the Old Ones." Angelique shook her head, not recognizing the reference, and Culdun nodded. "Few remember us. We were scattered. Some fled to the northern icelands. Some crossed the sea to try and begin again in the Great Forest. A few stayed, hiding scavenging like animals in the deeper woods. But mostly we crossed the dividing waters and sought a new way among your Continent's peoples. We were not well received. We appeared odd. We were too short for laborers. We were too clever to be trustworthy. With our painted bodies, we were seen as too heathen to be—"

"No," Angelique breathed in protest, gazing at the magnificent writhing coils of vines and snakes. "The work is beautiful. Surely beyond the metalwork crafts."

"Even the snakes?" he challenged boldly, turning his arms and flexing the tendons, to make the images seem to come alive.

Angelique offered a quizzical expression and sat back in her seat. "Why would someone not like snakes? I have come to respect the guardianship of a great many garden snakes, Culdun. I prefer stepping around them in the barn and fields as opposed to chasing filthy rats with my broom."

"These are not garden snakes, mistress," he warned softly.

"Ah, then I am mistaken? You are not here as my guardian?"

His lips curled slowly, and the soft laughter began again.

Angelique shared his smile, adding quietly, "There are a great many sorts of guardians, Culdun."

"And I am merely one with a different perspective?"

"So it would seem."

Chapter Four

Her sleep that night was fitful. Not from the rock and sway of the carriage, but rather from dreams. Aloysius' nervous eyes stared out of vine-latticed prisons as shimmering red and blue snakes guided her down a path, their bodies glowing as they kept the darkness at bay. But only until she reached the end of the road, and then there was nothing but a portal into blackness. And so Angelique welcomed the jostling which kept waking her. She was not prepared to find what that blackness was hiding.

For the most part, Culdun rode up top with the driver. He shared meals with her, producing lavishly filled baskets full of all sorts of cheeses, meats, and sweets. He lit the pink chimney lanterns at dusk, and once she even awakened to find a soft, quilted coverlet and satin pillow had been arranged around her for comfort.

She was touched by Culdun's concern, but the fact that he had not awakened her with his movements was alarming. After years of tending an invalid mother, Angelique knew only too well that she should have noticed the touch of Culdun's hand, but calmed herself by remembering that Culdun had spent many years learning to move this quietly. But as the next day wore on, Angelique began to admit that the little knot in the pit of her stomach was not simply nervousness. It was fear.

She was a fairly clever woman. It would have taken far less to draw her suspicions, especially where Aloysius' adroit use of half-truths was involved. But she had been preoccupied with the rational, typical sorts of things he might so conveniently overlook.

Now Angelique realized, much more than the usual details must have been neglected. Culdun was of a very different kind of person. In fact, she was now certain he was not quite mortal. She had to wonder at what sort of person could claim the loyalty of a folk who were not-quite-mortal. Her mind said it was likely a person who was not-quite-mortal himself. But what did such a person want with a very mortal bride?

Culdun's worry for her waning appetite and growing silence resurfaced at lunch. Again he had asked if she agreed with the terms of the proposal; it was not too late to be returned home. She had assured him that it was the anticipation she was finding difficult, not her regrets. When he left her alone, Angelique realized that not once had she considered returning to the dreary prison of Aloysius' house. Instead, her thoughts had been singularly absorbed with the fears of the mysteries to come — her fear that she would prove inadequate in meeting the challenges ahead. No, it had not been regrets which plagued her.

The insight lent some relief, and the rhythmic jostling of the carriage began to lull her into a less fretful sleep. The air was warm. The sun filtered cheerfully through the wooded ceiling that branched above the road, and for a short time she slept, feeling safe.

When Angelique woke it was to the sound of voices outside the carriage. Culdun's back blocked the door's window as he stood on the step, speaking to another on horseback.

At first, Angelique assumed they had simply stopped to change horses again. The lack of clink and clatter registered almost immediately, however, and she sat up, pushing back the thick swirls of her hair. Her silver comb had come out, she realized with a start, thinking she must be a disheveled mess! With relief she found it had not fallen far, and she ran it through her hair a few times, trying to get the worst of the tangle back into some order. Just as she began to fit the comb back into place, Culdun's words became clearer, and Angelique realized they were talking about her.

"...fine considering," Culdun continued. "The trip has been exhausting for all of us, yet she has not once complained. There is strength in her."

"Aye, it is easy to forget the exhaustion of distances. I am sorry to force you through such a long journey. You say she does well, though?"

Angelique liked the voice. It was low but not deep, and she edged closer to the carriage door. She wished Culdun would move or that she had the courage to open the shade on the other window.

"What does she know of me, Culdun?"

Angelique flinched at the emptiness in that quiet question.

"Very little, my Liege. Apparently her father was somewhat lax in providing details."

A bitterness twisted the other's laughter. "Had we expected him to be any different from the others? Shall we wager, Culdun, that he's said nothing of magick or perverted monsters?"

"She is different." Culdun's solemn words sliced quickly through the sarcasm.

"How different, Culdun?"

"She possesses... a different perspective."

Angelique smiled at the phrase. She had won an ally in Culdun. Whatever task lay ahead, he would be there with his support. And if he, with all his years of wisdom, believed in her, then perhaps she needn't question her own abilities.

Culdun shifted and Angelique glimpsed the white flanks of a tall, skittish horse. The animal danced away and its rider skillfully brought it around in a tight circle. All Angelique could see was a thigh clad in dark britches and a glossy black boot. A well-muscled steed with a competent, long-legged rider; she almost giggled at the contrast it provided to her pot-bellied, gout-legged fears.

"Settle Angelique in her room." The bite had left the words and a cautious tension had emerged instead. "Arrange for her meals if she has need."

"You'll not greet her today?" Culdun's tone was careful.

"Tonight at dinner. Eight as usual. As you say, it has been a long trip. She deserves a few hours at least to recuperate before being confronted with the wicked magickian, doesn't she?"

"You are overly harsh with yourself, my Liege."

"I am overly busy," the other corrected. "The poachers were out again last night."

"What? Was the moon out?!"

"Aye, one of our odd days. We slipped into their world

again, and they into ours. I'm off to unearth the rest of their traps before any of your village children do."

"Very well. I'll tell her what you're about."

"Do you think she'll understand?"

Angelique frowned at the implied mockery in the voice, but in her defense Culdun said, "My Liege, you have not met this sort of woman before. She is not like the others."

For one moment, there was silence, not even the horse's bit jingled. Angelique gathered her courage and moved to see around Culdun's shoulder. What she saw made her breath catch in her throat. A tall, strong figure sat motionless on a fine looking stallion, black-gloved hands holding a tight rein. The loose-fitting jerkin, belted at the waist, was as black as the shiny boots and made a sharp contrast with the whiteness of the shirt sleeves that billowed with the wind. A narrow, red cape draped about head and chest, rakishly flung back over one shoulder. With the way the cape hooded and hung, it was impossible for Angelique to see the other's face. The stallion snorted abruptly, shifting against the reins to protest the stillness. The rider held him easily.

"Is she pretty, Culdun?"

"Yes, my Liege."

"I might have been spared that, don't you think?" The emptiness in the rider's voice had returned.

The horse tossed its head impatiently. Suddenly, without another word, the rider spun the beast about and launched into a full gallop. Culdun climbed back onto the driver's bench, but Angelique barely noticed. She watched the horse and rider until both vanished from sight.

Angelique was a shaking mass of nerves by eight that evening. Her logic had been pushed to the brink of rationality, and her body regretted the exhaustive turmoil of the past night. Her corset was fashionably too tight. Her feet were protesting the persistent necessity of real shoes. But the dress, with its pearl-seeded, peach bodice and cool, ice-blue silk was the most beautiful thing she had ever been uncomfortably tied into.

She had wanted to meet Drew with confidence, not insecurity. But this palace was an endless torture of subtle reminders that she could no longer be quite sure of what she was dealing with.

How, for example, could each dress in the wardrobe be exactly her size? How could her haphazard words sometimes alter a ruby-studded hair comb into one with sapphires? And how could similar words change the color of her petticoats from cream to white? It was all terribly disconcerting. Somehow, she had never suspected that Aloysius' use of the term "magickal" should have been taken so literally.

Culdun had appeared just as she was preparing an elaborate excuse. He shooed her two attendants away, muttering something about silly nieces, and assured Angelique that she need take no notice of their silence; it was simply that they were more afraid of her than she was of this dinner.

A grateful smile answered his jest, and feeling slightly less adrift, Angelique followed him downstairs. After he left her in a parlor that was nearly as large as the ground floor of Aloysius' house, however, she again began to feel her insecurities rise.

She barely noticed the embroidered chairs and expensive carpets, so intent was she on keeping silent. Her odd habit of talking to herself had a decided risk in a place such as this. So she concentrated instead on the heat from the fire, trying to warm her chilled fingers.

She held the silver rose, ever mindful of its thorns, but unaware of its delicate beauty in the flickering light. She closed her eyes, pressing a hand to the flat of her stomach and forcing a few even breaths. Just when she felt she was beginning to relax, the sound of a voice startled her into nervousness again.

"Are you well, my Lady?"

The tall, cloaked figure stood a few steps inside the doorway, a dark shadow silhouetted by wavering torch light. The stance was a nervous one, as hands clenched and weight shifted uncertainly.

It had not occurred to Angelique until that moment that

Drew would also be nervous.

"I am well," Angelique managed. "Only somewhat nervous."

Fists uncurled and weight settled. "That is understandable. Forgive me if I startled you."

"You did not." Suddenly, she remembered who she was addressing and gathered her skirts to sink into a hurried curtsy, murmuring, "It is I who should beg forgiveness, my Liege."

"No!"

Angelique looked up without rising and waited. It was disconcerting to find that the cloak hid both shape and face of this stranger.

"Please." The other approached slowly. "Please get up."

Angelique rose, but the unspoken question of 'why' remained between them.

"I would prefer we dispense with such formalities."

"If you like." Angelique smiled.

Drew's swift intake of breath was audible, and Angelique glanced at the gloved hand that clutched the chair's back. "My Liege?"

"Culdun said you were pretty, my Lady. But he never mentioned the sheer beauty of your smile."

Her chin lifted defiantly as Angelique remembered the overheard words and the feeling behind them: that beauty was not necessarily cherished here.

"Now I have insulted you. I am sorry. I find my manners suffer from lack of practice."

Almost unwillingly, that brought another small smile. "Your elegant apology belies any rudeness, my Liege."

"Then you were not insulted?"

Angelique ducked her head, hiding the urge to smile again. The curiosity in that voice had been all too apparent, and she thought that interest could be to her advantage. Black-booted toes came into her vision, blocking her study of the carpet, and Angelique relented quietly, "No, my Liege. I was not insulted."

She raised her head, finally daring to seek the gaze of this noble.

She gasped, sharp and sudden, a hand going to her throat, and her companion backed quickly away.

The deep shadow hiding Drew's face was disconcerting. The stark contrast between white shirt and red cloak, which hung over Drew's chest and was flung back across the other's shoulders, was almost frightening.

Crimson threads, embroidered in glistening vines, were stitched into the black velvet jerkin. But the rest was unadorned darkness. The supple leather of the short boots, the shimmering satin of loose trousers, the vest, the gloves — all brought her focus back again and again to the empty black void where a face ought to be.

"Are you even human?" The words came out in a hushed, frightened whisper.

Drew's shoulders stiffened. The tall figure turned away. Trembling, Angelique watched, desperation growing into fear.

"I have been called many things. Some of them human, some — not."

"But," Angelique, denying the evasions, demanded, "are you a man?"

"No."

Angelique cried out. In her consternation she had failed to pay attention to the rose's silver thorns and they sliced into Angelique's fingers. The silver rose dropped, laced with blood, to the carpet.

Drew was beside her in two swift strides. Taking Angelique's hand in a gentle embrace, Drew massaged outward from Angelique's palm, and Angelique felt the pain diminish. With her free hand she wiped away tears, glancing up again at that darkness where Drew's face should be. The edges of that emptiness seemed blurred, and she was again reminded that this was a place of magick.

"You do have a face, don't you, my Liege?" Angelique ventured in a whisper. "The blackness is an... illusion?"

Drew's fingers paused for a moment then resumed their tender ministrations. "Yes, I have a face, if that's what's worrying you. Here now, is that better?"

Angelique stared at her palm, flexing her fingers. Neither

a trace of blood nor scratch remained. She bent and carefully retrieved the silver rose. A gloved hand covered her fingers again as she stood, and when it lifted, the crimson smudges were gone. The silver was sparkling and unblemished.

Her companion withdrew. Angelique felt guilt stir within her. She gazed at her hand and again at the rose. Her mother had been right: this was someone who knew tenderness. Yet she had offered only ignorant fear.

She grasped the tattered edges of her courage and came to stand before the hearth. Angelique could not blame the cowled figure for not acknowledging her, but it would have helped. She swallowed hard and offered, "I pray you may be patient with me, my Liege. I have had little experience with magick and — and with those who are not-quite-mortal."

For a moment there was no response, and then Angelique was rewarded with a soft, rich chuckle. "I see you have been talking with Culdun."

"Have I misunderstood him?" Angelique breathed, entranced by that soft note of laughter.

"No, you have not. May I ask what else my dear friend has said of me?"

Angelique thought of the laws against poachers and the sanctuary given to the Old Ones. "He said you are a man of a different perspective."

"A man of a different perspective..." The tone was once again hollow. The tension returned. "No, my Lady, I sincerely doubt that Culdun would ever have said I was a *man* of any sort."

"Forgive me!" Impulsively she laid a hand on the silk-clad arm, forestalling an abrupt move away. "But then what should I call you?"

Drew shifted uncomfortably and, blushing at her impulsiveness, Angelique removed her hand. "Now you find me too brash."

"No. Just... startling." The words were spoken in a whisper. "I am amazed by your courage, my Lady. Few women have ever dared touch me."

Angelique frowned, then resolutely placed the silver rose

in the palm of that black glove. "Has a woman not the right to touch the man who... the one who... " She stumbled over the words she feared would again cause pain. In frustration, Angelique repeated, "What shall I call you, my Liege?"

A breath, then two, passed and Drew slowly placed the rose on the mantel. "My name is Drew. I would be honored if you would use it."

"You are displeased with me?" Angelique gazed at the abandoned rose. "You're annulling our engagement?"

"No." It was spoken wearily, as was what came after. "I am merely uncertain if you know what you've agreed to."

"I will learn —"

"Yes." A sigh, a pause, then, "Learn you must, my Lady. For it will do neither of us any good if you... do not understand."

Angelique felt the weariness herself. Her head bent and, exhausted, she found herself close to tears.

"I have kept you from dinner —"

"No, please." Angelique shook her head. "It is not your company, my Liege. It is merely fatigue."

"Which has not been helped by my company." A mocking self-deprecation colored the words, but Angelique was too tired to argue. "You should be in bed, my Lady."

"Would you find it rude of me?"

"Not in the least." Drew;s voice was warm and reassuring. "Can you find your way?"

Angelique nodded and managed a small smile. "Yes, Culdun was very explicit with his directions. But thank you."

"No, my Lady — thank you." The tall figure bent over her hand in a low bow.

"None of that." Impatiently Angelique tugged on the black-sheathed hand as a corner of mischief resurrected itself within her. "I thought we'd agreed to dispense with such nonsense?"

Drew laughed, a genuine hearty sound, and Angelique withdrew, feeling better about leaving with that warm laughter singing in her ears.

Chapter Five

"Oh, drat it all," muttered Angelique, spinning about on her heel. Hands on hips, she stepped to the side of the corridor and eyed the sunny garden court below with frustration. The babbling of the fountain wafted upwards with the cool breeze into the white, arching halls surrounding it.

This part of the palace was built in a square about that small, marble-floored garden. Her bedroom was on the third level across the hall from the open archways. Culdun had said the library was one floor up and around the corner. The winding staircases between floors, however, left Angelique feeling disoriented as none of them began or ended in exactly the same place on each floor.

She was lost. She had discovered just how lost she was when she had attempted to retrace her steps. So far she had found an unused parlor complete with dust covers, an exquisite sewing room with a marvelous selection of silks and wool as well as an abundant supply of needlework patterns, and a guest bedroom in need of a thorough cleaning. What she had not found, however, were her own rooms and the library.

"Well, I suppose somebody will come looking for me eventually," she muttered, bending over the railing again with a determined expression. The potted shrubbery with the fluffy red stalks could just possibly be the same one she'd been admiring before breakfast. She leaned out a bit further to get a good look around the post and saw the hanging baskets of purple flowers in the arches a level down. If she figured correctly, her room should be directly behind them. "Which means," she said, turning around, "the library *should* be right behind me."

The wide double doors reached to the ceiling and were centered in the long hallway. A smaller, single entry was visible further along on the left, but this was the entrance that invited use.

With the anticipation of success, Angelique grasped both

handles and pushed the doors open. Relief mingled with delight when her eyes fell upon the tall, dark bookcases which flanked a wide oak desk. A pleasant breeze ruffled a sheath of parchment papers that were spread out on the desktop, and Angelique quickly closed the doors to stop the papers from blowing every which way.

With the great double doors shut, the little whirlwinds ceased and the papers settled. Sparkling sunlight and fresh air gently streamed in through the tall, open windows, bathing the desk with light that spilled like liquid gold down the sides of the polished oak and pooled on the gleaming floor boards. The familiar smell of leather bindings and book dust made her feel at ease and Angelique leaned back against the doors with a happy sigh. She had never seen so many books. Rows of shelves extended back into the shadows on the right, and they were filled with books and much, much more.

A small globe of stars, a brass sexton and a few other navigational tools she knew little about dominated one shelf, but just as she was about to move closer to explore, the slow tread of booted heels upon the wood floor stopped her. Glancing about, Angelique spied a small corridor to her left. At its end, she glimpsed the satin blue of a bed quilt and the elegant drapes of a canopy. Until this moment, she hadn't realized that the library was attached to personal quarters – and they looked as though they had been recently occupied.

Angelique, thinking quickly, folded her hands before her as her host appeared from the depths of one of the book aisles. Unaware of her presence, Drew, familiar cloak in place, bent over a book and paused beside the desk, a writing quill dangling from gloved fingers. Drew tapped the quill absently against the binding for a brief instant, then stopped.

Angelique coughed discreetly.

Drew looked up. "My Lady? What a pleasant surprise!" The book snapped shut as Drew turned to face Angelique fully. There was genuine welcoming warmth in Drew's voice.

"Good morning, Drew."

"It is a good morning. Are you feeling rested today?"

"Yes. Thank you."

The Unexpected

"May I help you with something?" Drew closed the book and placed it on the desk. Cautiously, Angelique's host advanced a few paces then halted. "Or have you merely need of some company?"

"I didn't mean to intrude, my Liege. Actually, I was looking for the library."

"Ah," the figure turned about, "you have gotten yourself turned around. Not an uncommon problem here." Drew paused and gestured to the pleasant room. "Although this may look like the library, you've found my study instead. The library is just opposite, on the far side of the courtyard."

Angelique blushed and stammered an apology.

"No need to apologize. I'm afraid it's all too easy when you're new. Especially with the way the staircases keep moving about."

"Moving?" Angelique felt her frustration return in a flood. "You mean those damnable things have been shifting about all the while?"

"Culdun didn't tell you?" The other stepped nearer again.

"No, Culdun didn't tell me. Do you know I've been lost for a good twenty minutes!"

Drew laughed, and Angelique glared rebelliously up into the dark, faceless void. "It is not funny!"

"No, you're right. It's not," the other admitted, but the smile did not fade from Drew's voice.

Exasperated, Angelique leaned against the door with a scowl.

"I am sorry, Angelique, but I have never seen anyone quite so unafraid."

Dubiously, Angelique looked up.

"Others have always seemed so reserved, intimidated. But you? You're annoyed!"

"Well," a rueful smile danced across her lips, "it *is* annoying."

A friendly silence enfolded them. The scuffling of Angelique's shoe hinted at her temptation to pout. She glanced at Drew quickly and then away, "You're still smiling, aren't you?"

"I'm afraid so."

She watched as the tip of her shoe appeared and disappeared beneath the hem of her skirt. "Do you think it's silly of me to be annoyed?"

"No. Actually," a gloved finger reached over to trace the swirls of Angelique's hair comb, "I was wondering if I dare give you a reason to become even more annoyed."

"What do you mean?"

"Mind you, it may only be my ignorance of current fashions."

Angelique's eyes widened as the gold comb was adroitly plucked from her hair and offered to her. "Did you wish to be wearing one gold and one silver comb?"

"No," Angelique breathed. She closed her eyes and tipped her head back against the door. "I suppose that I was thinking of gold when I put in this one and silver when I put in the other. I'm afraid I'm not very good at controlling my thoughts – it's hard enough to control what I say out loud!" She giggled at that and suddenly they were both laughing. "I warned you," Angelique said when they paused for breath, "I have no practice with magickal things."

"Then perhaps," Drew said, striving for a slightly more serious note, "I should give you a hint or two?"

"Please."

"The servants in the house are for companionship and to tend to the details of maintaining the palace and grounds. However, the actual work is done by magick. The palace itself is sensitive to your commands. Any time you say 'I need' or 'I wish,' the palace will respond. Although, if you said 'I'd like' or 'I want,' it would ignore you." Drew paused before adding, "I found the more I limited the specifics, the fewer accidents occurred."

Angelique blinked. "You built this place?"

Drew shrugged noncommittally. "Some of it. Mostly I re-designed it to suit my purpose."

"And what purpose is that, my Liege?"

There was a moment of hesitation, and then Drew answered, "To protect the lands and the village while I wait."

Angelique almost asked 'wait for what?' but something in

the rigid tension that suddenly gripped Drew's body stopped her. She raised her gold comb instead and challenged lightly, "Do you think I really could change it myself?"

The tension fled. Drew chuckled softly and waved a gloved hand. "Try."

Angelique took a breath, excitement stirring. "I need a silver comb." The gold twinkled and then it was silver. "I did it!"

"You did." The black-gloved hand passed over the comb, changing its design. A splay of diamonds now graced the scalloped ridges and then Drew murmured something.

Angelique stiffened as she felt her hair suddenly swept back into place.

"It does take some practice," Drew explained matter-of-factly. "If you want the comb's design to match, you need say so."

"And the staircases? I'm quite certain I said nothing."

"Then they wouldn't have known where you were going. The destination would be completely determined by whoever was on them last. The palace is limited by some physical boundaries. Often, when one stairwell is used, another must also move in order to compensate for the change."

"But I only wished to go up one flight. No matter where it left me off, I shouldn't have gotten so thoroughly twisted about."

"In this place you will never need to climb more than one flight of stairs. Whether you begin on the first or the third floor, you will take only one flight to reach the fourth."

A sudden breeze disturbed the desk's parchments, and Angelique was reminded that she had interrupted something. "I should leave you to your work."

"If you like." Her companion straightened. But Angelique hesitated, eyeing the little corridor to the bedroom. "I honestly didn't mean to intrude." She opened the door, but left her hand resting on the handle.

"Angelique." Drew's gloved hand folded over hers. "This is your home now. There is no place forbidden to you. You are welcome anywhere in the palace."

Overwhelmed by the sincere kindness in Drew's voice, Angelique blinked back sudden tears.

"Now I have made you cry." Drew's hand withdrew as if afraid of burning her. "I do not seek to hurt you, my Lady."

Angelique looked at Drew for a moment. "I am not frightened, my Liege. But if you show me such kindness, then you must expect a few tears of happiness." And with that, Angelique slipped quickly out the door before Drew had a chance to respond.

A polite cough drew Angelique's attention away from the book she was reading. Looking up, she swiveled around on the bench to find Drew standing behind her. The room's shadowed aisles seemed dense in comparison to the brightly lit area with tables and benches which lined the window wall. But Drew's cowled figure was recognizable even in the dimness.

"If you'd rather I go – ?"

"No. Not at all," Angelique insisted, smiling as the hesitation in Drew's stance was replaced with confidence.

"Again, you surprise me," Drew shared, nodding toward the book. "You read. I'd thought you'd be in search of a dress pattern or pictures."

Angelique made a face. "Aloysius taught me so he wouldn't have to read to Mama so often. Which was typical of him. He'd make you think he was doing you a favor, but it was always himself he was serving."

"Yet it was a gift after all, in the end, wasn't it?"

"Yes," Angelique admitted, then smiled. She opened the book to the place she'd marked with her finger and said, "I was reading about the Persian astronomer who was among the first to believe the world was round. It seems amazing to me that people were so certain once the world must be flat."

Drew placed a booted foot on the bench top and leaned forward to rest elbow on knee, hand dangling freely. "Very certain."

"It was extraordinary. He was virtually the only one to think that the Earth moved about the sun. He suggested that only the moon circled us. He suggested that there was a whole universe out there—"

"And that the world just couldn't possibly be flat."

"Can you imagine believing something that seems so obviously wrong to us now?" Her eyes widened as she stared off into space. "Such conviction that there was so finite a space that if one sailed too far, the ship would literally fall off the edge of the world and into oblivion."

"So ancient an idea must surely be foolishness," Drew teased gently.

"They couldn't have known any differently!" Angelique challenged, annoyed at the whimsical tone of her companion. "What evidence did they have to the contrary? They hadn't the means to prove their world was anything other than what they could see! It would be like standing atop this palace and seeing the valley as a whole, ringed by your tall brick walls and then, beyond, by the ranges of mountains. Why, the very hills look as if they hold the skies high! Why would anyone have had reason to question their senses?"

"They would have no good reason at all."

"Yet you're laughing at me."

"Not at all," Drew corrected cheerfully. "I simply find nothing strange in the idea that a world may be flat – or round. Have you ever wondered if it wasn't truly flat in the first place?"

Angelique eyed her companion dubiously. "I don't understand."

"Before we began to think in terms of science and proofs, do you think the world was round? Or was it flat once, just as so many believed it to be? Perhaps the discovery, the very act of proving it round, created the reality of it being round."

"But how can something be what it was not before?"

Drew waved a gloved hand and a pale rosebud on a thornless stem appeared. "How indeed?"

Angelique stared at the flower, eyes narrowed in concentration. "You're suggesting science has become the magick? In its process of discovery, there are elements of some sort of spell?"

"Is that true?" Angelique lifted the rose thoughtfully, her

gaze drifting upwards. "Or is it the mystery itself that is magicked away with the spell? Like the black veil of your face... is the truth hidden by some cloak until the spell, or the science, can take us beyond our fear? Perhaps the magick is the light that pierces our blindness and science merely our best method of challenging society's assumptions?"

Drew nodded, impressed, acknowledging the logic of her thoughts. Silence fell easily between them. After a moment, Angelique moved, offering the pale bud to Drew, who took it slowly. As the rose passed from Angelique's hand to Drew's, Angelique spoke a few words under her breath, trying a soft spell of her own. The bud opened slightly, releasing a faint, pleasant fragrance.

Drew lifted the fragile gift, relishing the sweet scent. "Thank you."

Angelique smiled hesitantly. Her eyes fell to the open page of the book. She closed it slowly and looked up at Drew.

"May I ask you a question?" she said.

Drew stiffened momentarily, but nodded.

"Are you not overly warm wearing that hood and gloves all the time?"

Drew relaxed and answered, "It's simple, really. I only have to say 'I wish to be comfortable,' 'I wish to be cooler' or something of the like, and the palace accommodates me."

"But outside?"

"Then I have the brisk spring winds." Angelique continued to stare at Drew as if she expected more on an answer, but when none was forthcoming, the conversation lagged. "Do you ride?" Drew asked suddenly, breaking the silence.

"Do I like to ride or am I a good rider?"

"Both."

"Yes, I like to. No, I don't ride well."

"A lack of practice?"

She nodded.

"Would you like to ride with me? We've a wonderful garden trail, shaded by trellises of a thousand different flowers. The breezes are always cool. There are a dozen fountains that will sing for you."

"It sounds beautiful," Angelique sighed, then caught herself abruptly. "There is a problem."

Drew sat, straddling the bench. "Tell me."

Angelique colored. "I cannot ride like a proper lady, my Liege."

There was a puzzled silence, then her companion admitted, "I do not understand. How does a proper lady ride?"

"Side-saddle, my Liege." And then she found herself hurrying to explain. "I learned as a child, you see. My eldest brother, Ivan, would put me up on our old plow horse and lead me around the courtyard for a special treat. It didn't seem to matter if my skirts bunched at that age. When I was older and I rode the old mare in from the fields after plowing, I was too tired to care about whether or not my petticoats were showing."

"And where was this eldest brother when you were doing the plowing?" The displeasure in Drew's voice was audible. "I did not know that tending the fields had become a daughter's duty." Drew's hand curled into a fist.

"Please do not judge them so harshly, my Liege. I did what I did as much for myself as for them."

"For your father?"

Her head bent and she whispered, "It was for Mama. To pay for what she needed."

"Did you come here for her sake as well?"

Angelique glanced up, the anger in Drew's voice had turned to gentleness. "In part," she answered honestly.

"And the other part?"

She straightened, folding her hands on the book. She forced a smile and stared straight ahead. "I couldn't quite bear what would become of my life if I didn't."

Drew reached out and covered both of Angelique's hands with one gloved one. Angelique, aware of the warmth in that touch, felt her breath catch when she thought again that this was the person she would marry. Her skin tingled and she felt her mouth go dry, as she wondered for the first time what that warmed leather glove would feel like cupped against her cheek and then, more boldly, what that hand would feel like against her skin.

"Would you *like* to come riding?" Drew pressed, withdrawing that hand slowly.

Forcing her mind to focus on the question, Angelique managed a nod.

"Then we go riding!" her companion announced, rising suddenly and pulling Angelique up as well.

"Like this?!" Angelique protested. She allowed herself to be dragged only so far toward the door. "But I can't!"

"Why not?"

"In these skirts? It's not practical!"

"Then we'll dress you differently." Drew waved a hand. A loose fitting tunic, its drawstring collar neatly tied, and a suede pair of breeches tucked into short boots replaced the troublesome clothes.

Angelique flushed, deeply embarrassed.

"You are not comfortable," Drew said. "I have offended you."

"Do you..." Angelique managed a small smile. "Would you prefer me as a young boy, my Liege?"

Drew cocked her head, acknowledging the gentle jibe. "I do not prefer men to women, if that's what you mean," Drew offered. "I was merely providing clothing more suited to riding. If you would rather—" Drew raised a hand as if to change Angelique's attire again.

"Drew, wait. I didn't mean to imply..." she faltered, then, after a moment added, "It's just that — I've never worn clothes such as these before."

"Angelique."

She glanced down at herself and then up at Drew. "Do you not find this terribly immodest?"

Drew shook her head in response. "You need not answer to the rules of outside society. It is your choice what you wear."

Angelique grinned crookedly. "Then if I can have anything, I'd like my old clothes. The ones I wore at home."

"Describe them."

"The blouse had short sleeves." She gestured to the middle of her upper arm. "I'd wear a laced vest instead of a corset. A simple skirt and petticoats." Angelique blushed at the thought of bare ankles anywhere outside of the muddy pastures or Aloysius' house. "They came below the knees a little."

"Done!" Drew's hands clapped together and Angelique gasped at the transformation. The silk blouse Drew had made was a summer-sky blue; her vest was of black felt, appliquéd with red and pink rosebuds; the petticoats were the softest cotton, covered by a dusky gray-blue skirt of fine light wool.

"Better?"

Angelique nodded, laughing breathlessly. "It's beautiful!"

"We will need to do something about those boots."

Angelique grimaced, realizing she was still wearing the short boots the breeches had been tucked into. "To tell the truth, I wish I didn't have to wear anything."

Angelique gasped as she realized what she'd just said. But Drew's hand was already in the air and, in the same moment that Angelique felt the warm breezes against her bare skin, Drew's red cape suddenly tied about her throat and slid down to cover her to her toes. She clutched frantically at its edges, realizing that she wasn't wearing a thing underneath.

"You meant not to wear anything *on your feet*, I think?"

Angelique nodded, still unable to speak. Drew obliged with a spell. Angelique felt the beautiful riding clothes – sans boots – once again appear. Her thoughts raced in desperate, unspoken questions.

"I saw nothing, Angelique."

She drew a breath, calmed her racing heart. "Thank you."

Drew sketched a bow.

Slowly, Angelique untied the cape and drew it off. She folded it over her arm. The satin lining was smooth, the crimson velvet soft beneath her fingers. "May I keep it, my Liege?"

A pause and then, "Of course."

Angelique stared at Drew, prompting the other to ask, "My Lady?"

"My mother would say you have more than a tender soul, my Liege," she said quietly. "She would say you have honor."

Chapter Six

The hairbrush paused as Angelique gazed into her mirror, eyeing the crimson cloak that now lay draped across the foot of her bed. How could Drew, who had been so protective of her, so abruptly seem to forget her existence? How could the one who had laughed with her over dinner, taught her backgammon and told such magickal stories have become so distant?

There was no one but herself to blame, she scolded. The touch of Drew's black-gloved hand had unsettled her, just as it had the first time she's allowed herself to think of what that touch might lead to. Only this last time Drew's touch, meant to be gentle and playful, nothing more than correcting the improper placement of a backgammon marker, had made her heart leap and her stomach flutter. Her own sudden feelings had frightened her. And so, startled by her own emotions, she had pulled away, wide-eyed.

For a long moment, the ticking of the corner clock had engulfed them, the only sound in a room which had moments before been filled with their laughter. Before Angelique could explain why she'd pulled away, Drew rose, slowly, almost wearily. "Forgive me." Drew's voice had been clipped. "I did not realize my touch was so offensive to you."

Startled, Angelique had been unable to recover her equilibrium before the Liege strode stiffly from the room.

A wall of tension had come down between them, a wall that had been kept mercifully at bay for a few days at least. Angelique could not yet fully identify the emotion that engulfed Drew during these moments – anger, perhaps, or sadness. Angelique had come to know only that any reaction from her that bordered on surprise – especially at Drew's touch – might as well turn Drew to stone.

The morning after, Culdun said Drew would be out attending to some local business for a day or two. By way of apology for the absence, Drew sent a bouquet of small pink and dusky blue flowers. "My Liege said you were most taken with the summer house where these were in bloom. If you like, you could take the mare out this afternoon. I'm sure my nieces would be happy to accompany you," said Culdun. But Angelique had refused. Somehow, without Drew, the prospect of riding didn't have the same appeal. Instead she haunted the library and the gardens close by the house, counting the hours until Drew would return.

But a "day or two" had stretched into eight. Then, even after Drew returned, her host had remained unavailable, even at dinner. Angelique, tormented by the belief that she had caused Drew such deep distress, fell into despair.

She bemoaned her clumsiness. How could she have been so ungrateful in the face of such gentleness and kindness? How could she have hurt the only person who had ever made her feel smart and beautiful and... wanted? Yes. Wanted.

She missed Drew's unsettling humor, even though it sometimes annoyed her, especially when Drew seemed to be laughing at her and not with her. But she only had to look below the surface of their interaction to see that was not so. Drew could never be so cruel. It was one of the qualities she had come to appreciate.

She missed Drew's quiet concern. And even though the thought of Drew's touch had startled her, Angelique couldn't bear to think that Drew would ever believe that Angelique was afraid of affectionate touch!

Angelique set the hairbrush aside resolutely. Enough was enough. If Drew was truly her betrothed, then she had the right to seek her Liege's company, did she not? Of course she did. Staring at her reflection in the mirror, she promised herself that, come morning, Drew's unavailability would change!

Angelique paced in the library, awaiting Culdun's return. After what seemed like an hour had passed, Culdun appeared in the doorway. He looked away for a moment and then his eyes sought her face. She knew even before he spoke what the answer would be. "My Liege regretfully declines the invitation to ride." Culdun's voice was quiet.

Angelique sank down into one of the overstuffed chairs and let her head fall into her hands. "Oh, Culdun, I've made a terrible mess of things. What shall I do?" she fretted anxiously. "How can I say I'm sorry if my Liege won't even let me say good morning?"

Culdun smiled in quiet sympathy. "I think, my Lady, there is need for fewer self-recriminations on both sides."

"But I am the one who failed, Culdun. My Liege trusted me to be different and I have failed."

"Have you thought," Culdun offered quietly, "that such a difference may be frightening in and of itself when finally found?"

Angelique considered this. "That had not occurred to me." Angelique paused a moment. "Do you think Drew is really too busy to come riding or is it this other matter which keeps us apart?"

"I do not know, my Lady. There were a fair number of parchments scattered about the study when I left."

"The study?" Angelique paused. Then she offered a small smile. "My Liege did say I was welcome to venture wherever I would in the palace."

A hint of a grin appeared on Culdun's face. "My Liege has indeed said you may go anywhere you'd like."

"Strange," she breathed, "I am overcome with a desire to see the study again. I think there is something in that room which will answer a question that has been puzzling me for days."

Culdun grinned openly now. Angelique moved past him and into the hallway, then turned toward the staircase and voiced her desired destination.

Her resolve wavered a little when confronted with the closed doors to the study. For a moment, Angelique hesitated, fingers toying with the laces on her green vest. Then abruptly she knocked and entered without waiting for an answer.

Drew, cowled as always, glanced up from the desk. A

wind rushed eagerly from the open windows, encouraged by the cross-draft created by the open door, and tugged at the edges of the red cloak and the corners of the parchment scrolls.

Steadying her nerves, Angelique closed the doors behind her and the draft died. She slowly walked the silent length of the room and halted a few feet from the desk.

There was a brooding challenge in Drew's form and something else, something darker and more menacing. "Why are you here, Angelique? I said I could not go riding."

"You said I was welcome to go anywhere in the palace I wished to go."

A pause. Then, "Why are you here?"

"It has been eight days, my Liege," Angelique began, her voice trembling a little despite her resolve. "I thought an apology was overdue—"

"An apology?" Drew interrupted harshly. Pushing back from the writing table, Drew all but sprang from the chair. The tall figure paced before the open windows in taut, clipped strides. "What have I to apologize for? Is the food not to your liking? The bed too soft or too hard? Has Culdun not seen to your every wish? What —"

"*My* apology," Angelique broke in, then faltered as Drew halted mid-step. She amended more quietly, "I wanted to apologize for my reaction the other night. I meant you no disrespect, nor did I mean to hurt you. I was frightened by what I felt when – when you touched me. Not by the touch itself. I never meant to insult your kindness, my Liege." She paused and then added, "I'm sorry."

"You have nothing to apologize for," came the terse retort, and the dark figure strode back to the desk.

"But –"

"Trust your instincts, Angelique. And be afraid. Now," Drew lifted the quill again, "you must excuse me. I have work to do."

Speechless, Angelique stood as if rooted to the floor. The curtness, the cold dismissal, was so unexpected. This must be some stranger, she reasoned, come to take Drew's place. This was not the person she knew.

"Go!"

She jumped, and moved to obey, fighting tears of anger and embarrassment. At the door she paused and looked back. Drew had not returned to work but was sitting, quill poised, as if listening for the door to swing shut behind Angelique. Suddenly inspired, Angelique murmured a word. Drew's quill disappeared and in its place appeared a pale pink rose, stripped of its thorns.

"What—"

Over her shoulder Angelique replied, "You said to trust my instincts, my Liege."

And then she was gone.

The fountain sparkled with silver droplets and tiny rainbows as the waters played and danced over the sculpted stones. Arching streams from winged seahorses and mounted nymphs tossed cool sprays of mist into the air. Drew sat at the fountain's edge, staring morosely into the rippled reflection which stared back. Uncharacteristically, Drew had pushed the cloak's hood back, but even the warm, honeyed sunshine could not dispel the despair within, The pink rose, Angelique's instinctual gift, lay on the fountain's edge. Drew's dark eyes caressed it again. The brilliant clearness of the sky, such a soft and even expanse of blue, the calls of half a dozen different birds, and even the warm, gentle breeze that lifted Drew's black curls went completely unnoticed.

Culdun appeared soundlessly, as always. "You wanted me, my Liege?"

"Yes." Drew's words came slowly, reluctantly. "When Angelique returns, please tell her... tell her I will be at dinner tonight." Drew looked up into the man's face, a thousand questions in the dark, haunted eyes.

But if Culdun had any answers, he did not offer them. "Yes, my Liege," was all he said. He bowed and was gone.

Chapter Seven

It was a quiet meal, each striving not to offend, not to assume, and yet Angelique was aware of the way her heart raced whenever Drew's soft voice emerged from the hooded darkness. She was aware of the pleasure she felt when her companion noticed the fit of her dress, the new style of her hair. And she became more determined not to disappoint.

After dinner, Culdun followed them into the parlor with a tray of brandy, but Angelique declined and wandered to the hearth. The fire was blazing and its warmth was welcoming in the night's unseasonable coolness. The silver rose still lay on the mantel and gingerly Angelique ran a finger along its stem.

"Take heed of the thorns, my Lady."

Angelique nodded, remembering their sting.

"We have not talked of much tonight, my Lady."

Angelique turned. "We do not always have to talk to enjoy each other's company, my Liege."

For a moment, Drew was intensely still, then suddenly in motion, moving with seeming casualness around the room. Angelique sensed that something was waiting to be said, but she would not hurry it.

"Why did you come here, my Lady?" Drew asked at last in a voice both hesitant and curious.

"I came in response to your proposal, my Liege. As I have said, I could not bear the thought of being scullery maid to my brothers' households should I fail to marry before they would claim me as their own."

"And if you had to make the choice again, knowing such magicks would surround you, would your decision be the same?"

"It would, my Liege."

Drew had come to stand at the mantel and reached out to touch the silver rose. Angelique held her breath at their sudden closeness. Taking the rose up in a gloved hand, Drew turned away, the hem of the cloak brushing against Angelique's bare hand. The woman shivered.

"Do you remember the terms of the proposal?"

"In exchange for my hand, you negotiated a business contract with my father."

"And?"

Angelique half-turned, but stopped herself. Instinct told her this was terribly difficult for Drew and if she turned to face her host, the other's words would dry up as quickly as a desert stream. She dropped her gaze to the carpet and, with forced casualness, turned back to her contemplation of the fire. To the hearthstones she said, "I had to agree to come here freely."

"Yet you could not have known what you were agreeing to."

"I knew what would happen to me if I stayed and, quite honestly, my Liege, I think — magick or no, not-quite-human or mortal to a fault — I have the better end of the bargain. My... Aloysius sees to his own self-interests, and if yours happen to coincide, then all is peaceful. But if not..." she trailed off. After a moment, she spoke again, "That Aloysius neglected to clarify certain aspects of the bargain was not surprising."

"You mean the magick?"

"That. And more. Aspects like yourself."

Despite the crackle and pop of the fire, Drew's sigh was loud in the room. There was the faint scent of rose petals, as if stirred by memory, and the silver rose reappeared on the mantel.

"You are to be Mistress of this house, Angelique. Regardless of marriage. I could never release you back to the care of one —" The words were bitten off sharply. "I am sorry. I know he is your father. But I could not in good conscience return you there."

"He is not my father," Angelique said abruptly, before she could stop herself, anger coloring her voice. She drew a sharp breath, suddenly mindful of what she had revealed.

"Not —?"

"He speaks for me as father," she amended, head bent. "But I am not his child. My mother had a lover. I don't blame her. I might have done the same if I'd found myself married to a man such as he. I've never met my real father," she finished quietly.

"And Aloysius knows this?"

She nodded.

"It does not excuse his behavior!"

"No, but I expect it made it easier for him to —" She broke off before more could be said. She had expected a different reaction than the concern Drew had shown her, and something inside her stirred at the feeling of protection Drew's words engendered. She finally finished with, "Parents are not always reasonable."

Drew's bitter laugh shattered her serenity, and she turned to face Drew for the first time since they had come into the parlor. "My Liege?"

"The time has come, my dear Angelique," Drew began, in a voice rich with sarcasm and something else Angelique could not quite identify, "to tell you of the true family Aloysius has sold you into!"

"Drew —"

"Contrary to Aloysius, my father was *always* reasonable. Ah, yes, a kind man. A generous one. He pampered me. Saw to my education. He doted upon me. For you see, I was his only child and he the only parent. He had his broad estate, his treasures — his power! He went unquestioned in his little domain. And so I grew to adulthood never knowing —" Drew broke off abruptly.

The air in the parlor seemed suddenly thick and close. Angelique stared at Drew, whose body was so full of angry tension that it seemed to set Drew's cloak to writhing like a living thing. Drew's breath rasped harshly behind the darkened hood. The clock ticked off the minutes.

Finally, Drew spoke again. "I never knew exactly what I was. But how could I? My *passions* were never challenged. I was his heir. It was that simple. No one would have ever dared to speak against —" There was another pause in which Drew seemed to fight for control. When Drew spoke again, the voice was softer, but far from calm. "Doubtless Culdun has told you of my step-mother and of her infamous skills as a witch?"

Angelique shook her head, "He said only that she came

into your life when you were older."

"Older, yes, but still very naïve. Naïve enough to fall in love, foolish enough to believe that love was meant for everyone. Including me. I was ignorant enough to the ways of the outside world. How was I to know that the love I bore for my stepsister was seen as sin?"

"Moral sin, my Liege? But how can that be if you were not related by blood?" Angelique asked, truly puzzled.

Drew did not answer, but continued as if Angelique were not even in the room. "I committed the crime of loving my stepsister. Two years younger, radiant with the joy of life. Just beginning to know what it is to be a woman. Just beginning to learn what love is about."

Drew paused and the broad shoulders straightened. "I had no right to pursue the trusting attachments of any young woman, Angelique. And yet I did pursue her. For a time, I even thought she returned my affections. Until the night we were discovered in the midst of our — *my* lusts. What I had thought to be her desire was fear... of me. What I had mistaken for love was merely —"

Drew's gloved hands gripped the back of a chair. The merciless rasp of self-hatred etched each phrase. "To see her terror! Her shivering in fear! Clutching at her dress as she begged her mother for protection! From me! My father's face, his revulsion, his horror as the truth was finally forced upon him.... It is all so clear to me still. Every image... every word said."

Angelique trembled. Icy fingers of fear pricked the skin on the nape of her neck. She stared at Drew with wide eyes, questions tumbling upon themselves in her head, warring to be released, but she knew better. She remained silent.

Drew seemed to be elsewhere, pulled back through time to that horrible night so many years ago. It all played out, just as it had then, and Drew was powerless to stop the rush of memories. Drew faltered. In the mind's eye, images spilled from memory and Drew was unable to stop them.

"*My daughter!*" the witch-woman screamed, emerald eyes burning like living fire, her black hair flying around her head like a thousand hissing snakes. "How dare you defile my own flesh and blood with your perverted touch?!"

Drew cowered, jerkin and tunic clutched in awkward desperation as she tried to hide her nakedness. Helpless and confused, she shook her head. Her disheveled tangle of ebony hair shimmered in the lantern light. She burned with shame.

"What have you to say for yourself?" The Count's words were flat with judgment. How could she explain to him that he encouraged what she was? Allowed her to think of herself as his mirror image, his son, his heir? He had never told her that women were only for men's beds and she had not assumed such a narrow view. But now his voice was full of rage. Where were the tender words meant just for her? The nicknames, the shared laughter? Where was her father? The man who stood before her, demanding and inflexible, was not the Count she knew. This man's words were judgmental and harsh. As if she should have known, somehow, all that was expected of her but never said. "Speak!" he commanded.

"I meant no crime, Papa! I love her," she cried, the truth of her words apparent to any who would listen. "As she loves me. I thought to marry —"

"No!" the shriek came as one from daughter and mother.

"I never loved you," screamed the girl as her mother moved to shield her more completely. "How could you imagine something so horrible? So untrue?"

"But you said —"

"Don't listen to the lies—" the daughter broke in. But the mother needed no convincing to prove the innocence of her child.

"Filth — liar! Marry my own to one of Nature's most warped abominations?" She spit on the ground in disgust. "If you were not my husband's child —!"

"I have no child but yours, wife," he said.

Drew whirled on him in stunned surprise. "Papa!"

He would not hear, but instead turned away.

"Father!"

At the doorway, he paused, but did not look back.

"Father, please —" The plea became a cry, a wail of despair that drove the girl to her knees as her father took one step away from her, and then another.

The witch stepped near, and from her lips fell the words of an incantation already begun, "...my daughter to protect and for all the daughters of those you have sworn to protect...." Words tumbled over each other like pebbles in a rockslide, erasing all in their path. Smoke rose. The witch circled the sobbing young woman on the floor. "...Hear me now and mark my words!"

The wind shrieked; the witch's cry rose to guide the gale. "Then find you a prisoner for your precious love! You shall be bound by spells and time in a place befitting such noble dreams. You shall be, oh swine of humankind, bound to a mockery of love which will play with you. Marry you say? Then marry you will. Love you say, then love *she* must! A maid as plain or fair as you choose. But *choose* she must! Freely and knowingly must she choose to marry you and consecrate those sacred vows in your monstrous bed!"

The gale reached its final fury, whirling around the crumpled form of the once-cherished child. The witch's final curse screamed over the howling wind:

<blockquote>
"Cast thee gone!
Beyond thy Death!
Cast thee out!
Doomed in Quest!
Beyond mere Time!
Eternity
Now...
is...
Thine!"
</blockquote>

"My father," Drew said at last, "roused by my stepmother's shrieks, found me in the barn with my stepsister. I tried to explain to him – to them all – that I loved her and she... she denied my love. My father, saying I was no longer his child, turned his back on me. And my stepmother... Her words were the most devastating of all. The witch-woman cursed me." Drew looked up at Angelique and repeated her stepmother's words, ending with the curse.

Silence hung over the dark parlor. The fire had ebbed to mere coals. Angelique shuddered. Her hands pressed to her chest. She felt faint. What had Drew just told her?

"And now, my Lady thinks there must be some error — some noble oversight. But there was none, I assure you. I wish only that my appetites reflected gentler passions!"

"But each of us may be only what we are," Angelique choked out against the strangling dryness in her throat.

"And what am I? I hear your desire to ask even though your fears urge you to silence!"

"Would you not have me know the one I would marry?"

"Who? Or *what*, my Lady?" The acid in Drew's voice burned. "Are we demons not all alike? Is it not enough to know we are demons?"

Angelique, frightened by the rage that swirled in the room as powerfully as the witch's windstorm, fought for control. Drew seemed like a serpent ready to strike and she a helpless creature caught in its mesmerizing stare. Words evaded her tongue. The silence deepened. Ashamed of her inability to speak, Angelique tried to choke out an apology, but found her throat closed by tears.

"Go to bed, Angelique." Drew's voice cut through the tension like a knife and fell away. The room was suddenly ordinary again, and Drew was nothing more than the bleak, hooded figure, half-hidden in shadows. In a flat voice, Drew said, "Go to bed and dream of dancing and stars and happy things. There will be no marriage between us."

She should have stayed. She should have protested. But Angelique could only run.

The night wind howled like a tormented animal. Angelique shivered uncontrollably in the emptiness of her great bed. Neither the fine lace and satin sheets nor the thickness of the eiderdown quilts did anything to ease the chill in her heart.

She could not imagine ever doing anything so terrible as to cause her mama to disown her. Her mama's love transcended all transgressions, no matter how wicked. Of that she was sure. But that was exactly what had happened to Drew. To be banished by the only family you had known simply because she had loved? It didn't seem right somehow. Angelique shuddered. She struggled to make sense of all that Drew had told her, but the words only echoed within her mind.

A crack broke through the howling winds. For an instant, complete, eerie quiet descended. Angelique sat bolt upright, heart racing. That had been the shot of powder and ball! Poachers!

Slashing torrents of rain struck suddenly at the window. Lightning flashed, illuminating the darkened night, and thunder followed close behind, crashing across the sky. Voices boomed abruptly in the courtyard below: Drew, Culdun and others.

Angelique snatched the red cloak from the foot of her bed and pulled open the doors to the terrace. Drenching, icy waters pelted her, the force of the rain hard against cloak and hair, stinging her face. The scream of Drew's white stallion cut through the night, and she ran for the terrace's stone steps, unmindful of her bare feet.

"Go back!" Drew shouted at her, looking fierce and dangerous high upon the stallion's back. Angelique's eyes strained to see through the night and the storm. Tying down saddlebags and readying the bridle, Culdun and two other Old Ones turned to see Angelique standing half-soaked and barefoot in the rain.

"My Liege!" Angelique's voice lifted above the thunder's shout, "you must not go alone!"

"Inside!" The mighty stallion lifted, his war cry shrill.

"The beasts are panicked. They will flock to the palace grounds and *I will not have you harmed!*"

"But Drew —"

"*Inside!*" Thunder flew from Drew's hand and, abruptly, Angelique found herself back in her room. The doors were fastened tight, though they rattled in the wind. She tried the handles, but they remained fast. She urgently rubbed the mist of her breath from the glass, straining to see into the black depths. Lightning spiked down and she glimpsed horse and rider. Then all vanished into the darkness. She waited anxiously for the next bolt of lightning. But when it came, there was nothing left to be seen.

Culdun came in search of Angelique later, half to assure himself of her safety, she guessed, and half to offer reassurance. But he did not expect the near-frozen figure he found.

Still dressed in the wet cloak, dark hair straggly and pale skin chilled almost blue, Angelique sat curled on the floor beside the doors. Her eyes were round, unseeing, haunted. She made no response when he spoke to her, but merely stared through the glass and into the storm.

Chapter Eight

"Culdun?"

"Yes, my Lady?" The little braid flopped across his cheek as he glanced up sideways. He was busy turning the mulch and soil beneath a rose bush. He smiled as Angelique folded her loose skirts and knelt beside him to help, approving of her practical way of dressing and matter-of-fact pursuit of such pleasures as gardening.

"The day we met, you invited me to ask questions."

"I remember, my Lady."

"May I ask a few more?"

Something in her tone warned these would not be simple questions. With a stiff grunt he got to his feet, and they moved the mulch bucket to the next bush. "Some of your questions I may not be able to answer, my Lady. There are oaths I have taken. But ask and we shall see."

"What does Drew hide behind the—"

"Ah!" Culdun sat back on his heels, shaking his head with a sad chuckle. "What shape? What form? What monstrous abominations do cloak and glove hide?"

Quietly, evenly, Angelique countered, "I need to know, Culdun."

"You have heard the story. Is that not enough?" His answer was evasive and they both knew it. She had heard but a fragment of a story, nothing more.

Angelique looked at him steadily. "If it must be, yes." She sighed and stabbed the trowel into the dirt. Leaning into the work, she continued, "It seems I am a fool, Culdun. Every time my Liege presents another bitter piece of history, I fall to pieces. When we are simply together, I am quite comfortable. But when confronted with that rage –" Angelique broke off with a baffled shake of her head.

"It is often easy to deny one's fears until confronted, my Lady. Your presence here has caused my Liege to again confront the pain of familial betrayal and the hope that your presence has engendered. It is not surprising that you would feel the power of that anger and that hope. And be frightened by it." His voice was quiet.

"It is cowardice," she retorted heatedly. "I should have been stronger. But Drew's tale was so full of bitterness and hatred, I was overwhelmed. I didn't realize until later just how much I'd succumbed to Drew's own horrors. I fled as if the fearful darkness of all that hatred was rising up to swallow me whole."

"And now, my Lady?"

"Now?" Her lips twisted. "Now I am angry."

Culdun's face showed his surprise.

"Not at Drew," she added quickly. "Never at Drew." After a moment she continued, "How old was this stepsister, Culdun?"

"Nineteen, my Lady."

"And who became the Count's heir?"

"The son born to the stepsister, my Lady."

"Tell me," Angelique growled, "has no one ever thought nineteen is a bit old for even unmarried girls to be quite so innocent?"

"Meaning?"

"I question the witch-woman's ambitions. Have a spouse plant enough suspicions and even the most loving parent can fail in the moment of crisis. I can imagine the bespelled words of a witch might only make the situation worse."

"I have often wondered if my Liege was not the more innocent of the lot."

"It seems plain that the Count's second wife wanted to ensure that her offspring would find favor over Drew. If that were the end, she might have used any means at her disposal to guarantee it."

"That would be a logical conclusion to draw, given the circumstances," Culdun agreed.

"And yet Drew not only doesn't see that possibility, but insists on shouldering all the blame as well!"

"It has always been so, as long as I have known my Liege."

Both fell into silent contemplation as they moved on to

the next shrub. Then Angelique pressed, "Has there ever been an attempt to break the curse, Culdun?"

"There has, my Lady."

"Tell me."

"There have been several young women. All have come here of their own free will, though none seemed too interested in my Liege or living here. They all departed after a time. Most commonly, a young man would be found wandering near the gates and brought in as Aloysius was, to stay for the night. His fancy would be taken with the mistress, hers with him, and my Liege would arrange for a dowry and the lady's departure. The only exception I recall involved a young lass who had been traveling with her brothers. Highwaymen struck the lads down, but her horse was swifter than the brigands'. She and her poor beast stumbled through our gates nearly spent. It was lucky for her that there was a new moon that night."

"A new moon?"

He looked at her. "You've noticed that the moon does not follow her normal course here, haven't you?"

Angelique shook her head. "I've had no cause to be outdoors after dark until last night."

"Ah, so then you don't know." He paused as if gathering his thoughts. After a moment he continued, "This place has its own cycles. Although you grow a day older when the sun rises, then sets, time moves differently here than it does in the outside world. Most nights there is no moon at all in our skies and the two worlds are not in phase. It was part of the witch's curse. But, though it is unpredictable, for whatever reason on some nights the worlds become one for a few short hours, and then the cobblestone road from the gate to the palace is open."

"And the poachers come?"

"No, my Lady. They need the moon to see by. They come on those nights that are rarer still, the nights when our worlds are so much in phase that a round, full moon rises in our sky. We never know when these nights will occur but we must be ever ready. Always remember: if you are ever out after dark and see a moon rising, best come in quickly. Those are the nights that bring poachers with their traps and their guns. And they always stir the forest animals into panic. Those nights are not safe, my Lady. Not for any of us."

"And yet my Liege rode out alone."

"Not alone, Mistress. With magic as powerful as any mortal could ever behold. My Liege is the only one who could dare to ride out as our protector."

A wry, little smile curled her lips as Angelique sat back, staring at the trowel in her hands. "There could not be much monster in one who would risk life to defend us all."

"That is true, Mistress," he answered. "But you should know, my Liege is cursed beyond the edges of death. Pain or crippling are still heavy risks, but until my Liege is wed, there will be no possibility of peace in death."

"No possibility at all? Like you, Culdun?"

Culdun responded with a deep, rumbling chuckle. "You'd like me to be immortal, my Lady?"

"Not-quite-mortal is different?"

"Very. My folk know the lure of the faery lands well enough. We can dance back and forth through that thin veil all our lives until, one day, the wine is too sweet and the music too pretty. And then we – just stay. But I do admit, it is a time of our own choosing, and we are a long-lived folk in the meanwhile."

"So Drew couldn't choose death even after hundreds of years? Even if desired?"

He nodded sadly. "The curse took that choice away."

"Yet if Drew were to marry, that would change?"

"Something would change, though exactly what is not clear. The palace exists because of the curse, but it is not dependent on it any longer. Over the ages, my Liege has acquired much power in the magickal arts, far more magick than the witch-woman might ever have expected. But would breaking of the curse mean all this would disappear? Or if the curse were broken, and my Liege wished to leave, would this place then cease to exist?" Culdun only shrugged.

"What would become of your folk, then?"

"Ah, what of us?" Culdun mused. "We have talked of it. We agree. We would never wish this timeless prison on our friend for even a second longer than must be. It would be no hardship for us to simply cross into the faery mists. Life here has been good to us. Then again, " Culdun nodded at his own thoughts, "the sort of woman who would wed our friend may not be the sort who would want to return to her family's home. We Old Ones have an acceptance for differences that I've noticed your Continent doesn't always practice."

Angelique could only agree with a solemn nod. She couldn't imagine the protective, gentle Drew among those such as Aloysius and her brothers.

"But enough of this melancholy talk." Culdun brushed his hands against the material of his trousers. "Last night, the poachers were driven back once more and today is a new day. Let us remember the beauty of the rose's bloom and not dwell upon the thorns."

When Culdun brought word later that Angelique would be dining alone once more, a soft curse hissed just under her breath.

"Culdun, might I trouble you to return a reply?"

"Most certainly, my Lady?"

Culdun waited patiently while Angelique composed a response. They shared a smile as she said, "Please tell my Liege that unless my Liege is ill, I expect my betrothed to pay me the common courtesy of dining with me. *Every evening.*"

"Yes, my Lady." He turned to go.

"And Culdun," she added.

Inclining his head, he acknowledged, "Yes, my Lady?"

"If, by chance, my Liege does feel ill, I will present myself as a bedside attendant and companion."

He got as far as the door this time before she called again. "And—"

They both bit back laughter now.

"And," Angelique continued. "I'm going riding. There is no need for you to bring me an answer as I will be quite unavailable until dinner."

"I will relay your message, Mistress," Culdun replied, still smiling. And with that, he slipped through the doorway and was gone.

"It's nearly dark, Culdun. She's never been this late, you say?"

"Never, my Liege."

Drew's slim-fingered hand rubbed at aching muscles in shoulder and neck. The tall, cloaked figure stared indecisively out of the study's window. Twilight was settling its thin, bluish veil across the garden below, and the splashing fountain of nymphs and seahorses was slowly fading into murky gray shadow. "I should have given her a talisman sooner. Then we would know if she were simply tucked away somewhere awaiting for me to appear for dinner."

"It is possible. She was quite determined not to give you a chance to argue."

"What makes you so certain she's not on the grounds, then?"

"She bathes at the same hour every night. It is a ritual she enjoys, or so my nieces say. Since it's well beyond that hour now, my Liege, I felt that I should tell you."

Drew turned from the window. "I dare say at Aloysius' she never had time for even such small pleasures." There was a wry smile in that voice. "Thank you for looking out for her, Culdun." Then, "We'd best send someone into the village to ask for word of her. Perhaps some of the children saw her riding out in the forest. Or else some of the farmers might have seen her."

He nodded. "I'll send someone right away." Halfway to the door he paused and added, "It may be nothing, my Liege."

Drew nodded faintly. "You're probably right. Let's wait until dinner before we really panic, shall we?"

Culdun was taken aback at the gentleness of Drew's humor. He could not remember the last time Drew had laughed without bitterness.

"Still, send someone now to the village."
"Of course, my Liege."

Angelique felt dizzy. The world around her was misty with twilight yet swirled like a waltz. Someone pushed another cup of wine into her hand with a merry giggle, and Angelique smiled, thinking she ought to have refused. But the music was playing again, and the harp and pipes were so lively. More laughter filled her ears and her companions, maids and youths seemingly as young as she, were urging her to down the cup so she might join the dance again.

The pale-leafed trees at the clearing's edge shimmered in the misty, blue-white air. The center fire leaped high, and the lithe figures gaily jumped the flames, moving in and out of the fire's glow as they danced. From one set of hands to another Angelique was passed, spinning and gasping.

Coldness crept in as full darkness descended, and Angelique thought she must be leaving soon. But the sparkling dark eyes of yet another pair of dancers bewitched her, and she gave in to the temptation of another round. Laughing, her dark hair flying, she took their hands. Their skin was cold as death in her grasp.

Angelique struggled to shake the cobwebs from her head. So tired. Sleep beckoned, aided by the soft pillow of a maiden's lap. Cool fingers stroked her sweaty brow, and Angelique smiled. A slender man, with bright dark eyes in a narrow, fine-boned face, sank down beside her with a cup.

The wine was chilled and sweet. It slid down her throat like crisp, cold water, and Angelique thanked him with a smile. She fought sleep, tingling all over with the icy touch of evening's air against her flushed skin. Her clothes felt heavy – binding –

and her hand pulled listlessly at the lacings on her vest.

The maiden upon whose lap she reclined smiled tenderly, and Angelique felt the woman's fingers leave off their light stroking of her brow to loosen the knot that held the vest together. A hand took her own, and Angelique glanced again to the youth beside her. He smiled, leaning closer. *He's going to kiss me*, Angelique thought, feeling nothing but a faint sense of surprise, and then understood that this was only to be expected.

As Angelique stared at the youth, a hand settled on his shoulder. Startled, he halted. Then that sparkling joy returned to his eyes as he recognized the newcomer. There was something familiar about the stranger, Angelique thought. But she couldn't quite place what it was.

Then suddenly she knew. She recognized the tapered lines of that hand. Only usually it was sheathed in black. But not this time. Angelique moaned as she felt the touch of that hand to her skin for the first time.

"Angelique!" The voice was sharp. She tried to speak, but her tongue felt heavy as a stone in her mouth. She groaned instead and struggled to focus her eyes.

"Angelique!"

"Don't be angry—" she mumbled faintly, barely able to force her eyes to stay open. Everything was a swimming blur. "I wouldn't have been late for dinner."

"I'm not angry." The words were soothing now and Angelique relaxed. Drew's arms slid beneath her, lifting her from the cool grass. She made a soft sound, snuggling against Drew's solid warmth, and lifting her arms so she could slip them around Drew's neck.

"I'm so cold." She was shivering now. A cold deeper than a midwinter storm stole into her. Her teeth began to chatter, and she pushed against Drew's sheltering heat.

"It's all right. We'll be home soon."

But it wasn't all right. She felt numb and groggy, but below the disorientation, fear was starting to collect in her belly. "Drew—" she began, but the rest of her words were choked by sobs. She felt a momentary sense of being elsewhere, suspended in time and space, alone and unsheltered. She tried to cry out, but before her voice could find expression, she opened her eyes to a familiar scene – her own room.

The lamps were lit and a fire burned in the hearth. Culdun's face swam into view as did those of his two nieces. They fussed around her. In a moment, she was bundled into woolen nightclothes and surrounded by a thick comforter. Culdun guided a brandy glass to her lips. "All of it, Mistress," he urged.

She choked on the fiery amber but didn't protest. Its sting made her feel real.

"Now, put her before the fire," the Old One ordered, and once again Drew's strong arms enfolded her, quilt and all. They settled on the floor at the foot of the grand bed. Angelique leaned into the embrace, burrowing into the bulky eiderdown. After a moment, her teeth stopped chattering and the ache in her chest eased as panic receded. Culdun knelt to peer at her. He gave a satisfied sort of nod and touched a rough knuckle to her cheek. "You gave us quite a scare, my Lady. How did you come to be in that place?"

"Not now, Culdun," came the quiet command from above her head. "There'll be time enough for questions later."

"True," Culdun agreed, and smiled. He touched her cheek again and then was gone, taking his nieces with him.

"Are you warmer?" Drew asked.

"Yes, but please don't leave me." She took hold of the arms that held her. "I couldn't bear to have you leave."

"I won't."

Exhaustion and relief flooded Angelique. Again she found her eyes closing, but this time there was no deathly chill, only the warm glow of the fire and the safe haven of Drew's arms.

"I'm sorry I missed dinner," Angelique mumbled.

"I was beginning to think you'd forgotten."

"How could I forget when I'd made it so plain that you were not to be excused?"

She was rewarded with a soft chuckle. Then, "Sleep now."

"Are you sure it's safe? Sometimes with frostbite..." she began, but found her thoughts were muddled, and she could not pick up the thread of what she'd been saying once she'd stopped.

"You're safe now."

"I'm still cold."

"You will be for a while. I'll stay with you."

"Protecting me again." She nestled down further into the quilt. "Thank you for coming after me."

A brief tightening, a hug, was the reply.

"Drew?"

"Yes."

"You will be at dinner tomorrow night, won't you?"

"Tomorrow and every night. I promise."

And then Angelique slept.

The whisper of faery music curled around Angelique's dreams. Like foggy little wisps, tendrils of joy and enchantment teased the corners of her awareness, coaxing, luring her back into that fey land of delights.

She could feel Drew's arms about her, but whether or not she dreamed the embrace she could not tell.

A feathery kiss brushed her temple. Then she felt her hand lifted and held. She murmured in surprise – Drew's hands were still gloveless!

The taste of the faery wine seemed to linger on her lips, and Angelique chased the sweet taste with the tip of her tongue. A finger rose to touch where her tongue had just been and Angelique shivered at the sensuousness of the touch.

She heard the faery music again and for a while, it seemed, she drifted. She could feel Drew's fingers on her skin, tracing the curve of her bottom lip, moving to cup her cheek and then straying back again.

Feeling playful, she nipped and caught the fingertip. It stilled obediently. Holding it lightly between her teeth, she passed the tip of her tongue over the rounded end and was rewarded with a muffled groan and a shiver. She let go and the hand slid to her chin, tilting it up and back.

Angelique struggled to open her eyes, but everything

seemed distant and out of focus. She could see a dark tumble of hair framing a face she could not quite discern.

Reaching up, Angelique freed her arms from the quilt's embrace and pulled Drew toward her. Her fingers tangled in the curling tangles at the nape of Drew's neck and she delighted in the feel of the silken softness against her skin.

She felt Drew's breath warm on her cheek and then the breath caught in her throat as Drew's mouth captured her own.

Faery tunes seemed to whirl about them as the kiss deepened.

A starry dust of silver and gold sparkles encircled them. Angelique felt herself lifted and laid flat upon the downy quilt. Drew seemed to be everywhere at once, above her, encircling her. She groaned as Drew broke off the kiss reluctantly, and arched into Drew's willing hands which sought the laces of her vest—

Angelique woke with a gasp.

She blinked, disconcerted. Then the quiet click of a latch drew her attention, and she glimpsed the retreating figure as her bedroom door was softly pulled shut.

Angelique took a deep breath. Her heart gradually ceased pounding as the last images of the dream began to fade. She was alone in her bed, the fire still blazed in the hearth.

It must have been a dream. It must have.

She could no longer fight the call for rest. Unable to resist, she fell back into sleep and into her dreams.

Chapter Nine

One of the combs slipped again, and with a resigned grimace Angelique pulled it free. The tumbling mass of hair spilled forward over her bare shoulder. She frowned at the golden hairpiece, trying to discern what was wrong with its design. Everything seemed right. Without much hope that it would stay long, she lifted her hair from her face and slid the comb back into place for the third time.

"My Lady."

Angelique smiled at Drew's deep bow, and, hands still busy with her hair, she dipped a small curtsy. Her eyes grew bright with teasing mischief. "Such formality, my Liege?"

Sweet laughter was the reply and Angelique's heart skipped a beat.

"I see you are feeling better."

"Yes, thank you."

"But somewhat light-headed?"

"Just a bit."

"The effects of the faery wine tend to linger. Doubtless you will dream of their music again tonight."

Angelique blushed. "It was beautiful music."

"Yes." There was a hesitant pause before Drew added, "but the memory of that beauty pales next to your own. If I may be so bold, my Lady – you are breathtaking tonight."

"Thank you," Angelique murmured, smoothing the satin and velvet skirts. The deep midnight blue sparkled with bits of gold thread. It had reminded her of the starry, moonless sky of this magickal world. She had chosen the dress especially in hopes of gaining just such a compliment.

Drew moved closer and a gloved hand lifted, almost daring to touch her cheek. But Drew hesitated and began to move away, but Angelique caught the hand with both of her own. Drew became still. For a moment, neither moved. Angelique turned Drew's hand over, opening the curled fingers. "Last night you wore no gloves."

"There are no disguises in the faeries' land," came the quiet reply.

"I remember nothing but your hands."

The cloaked figure nodded.

"They are very beautiful. And," she paused, looking into the shadow of Drew's hidden countenance before adding, "gentle. Must you hide them?"

Drew hesitated, then answered in a strained voice, "The gloves are as much for my sake as for yours, Angelique."

"Do not hide your hands from me for either of our sakes, Drew."

There was no reply. Then, "As you wish."

Magickally, the black leather dissolved, and the warm silken skin of Drew's hands made her gasp. She brushed her cheek against the softness and felt the tremor she caused both of them. Her eyes were tender with concern, and earnestly she pressed, "I am not like the others, Drew."

"I know." Drew gripped Angelique's hand more firmly with one. "Last night, when I found you had wandered into the faeries' mist, I feared I would be too late." Whispering words, Drew pulled something from the air. "Will you wear this for me?" Drew displayed a locket.

"Of course."

It was a thin piece, made of gold; the scrollwork, exquisite. Drew slipped behind Angelique to fasten it about her neck. The chain felt delicate, but it held tenaciously, and Angelique realized it was made by magick.

"It is a talisman for your safety. If ever you are out of the palace and have need, use this to summon me." Angelique pried the small catch open. Printed inside in a delicate script were magick words that Angelique did not know. "Hold it and call for me. I will know where to come."

"Will it summon you even through the faeries' mists?"

"Through fey dreams or mountain storms, it will reach me."

Angelique nodded, shivering faintly at the memory of the faery world. "Tell me, is it true I almost died last night?"

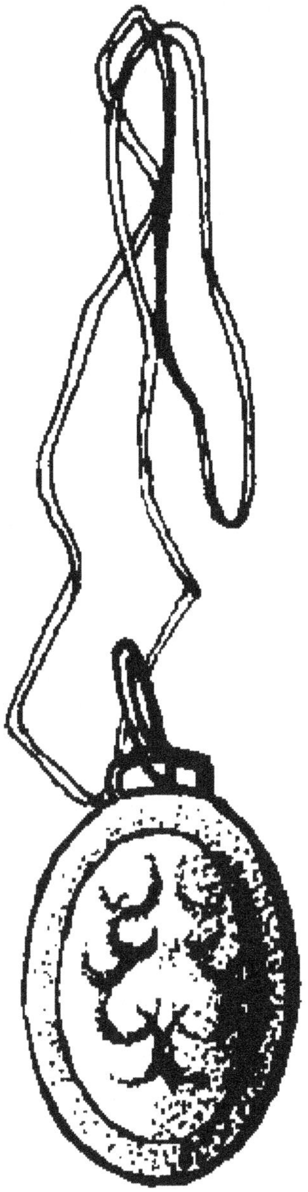

Drew nodded solemnly.

"But how? Culdun told me his folk often dance with the faery folk and yet seem unaffected. And they choose to pass into the faery lands after death?"

"Angelique, the faery lands are part of death's netherworld. The Old Ones have never been as limited to either world as mortals are. They have always been welcome in both. When they came here after many years of exile, they found the faeries' mist sought them out again. The mists ring their village now, hiding and protecting it from poachers and wolves alike. For them, it is like a castle's wall. As Culdun says, they walk among the faery folk freely, coming and going until—"

"One day the wine is too sweet and the dance too merry."

"Then they merely stay. But you are mortal, Angelique. Any mortal who passes through the misty boundary has very little time before the faery world claims her forever. Most do not even understand where they are soon enough to leave."

"I think I understand," Angelique said. "With the wine and the music, it seemed there was no need to hurry."

"And I could not let you go so soon, my Lady."

There was something in that voice which made Angelique reach out and grasp Drew's hands again earnestly. "I did not want to die, Drew. I simply did not understand that I was not to remain there. Until you arrived."

Drew, releasing Angelique's hands, cupped her face tenderly. Angelique held her breath as Drew came near, so close that Angelique could almost feel the sweet caress of Drew's warm breath on her face.

The dinner chimes rippled lightly.

Drew started and jerked back to awareness. Angelique felt Drew's hand fall away from her face and the tenderness was replaced with the familiar tension and awkwardness. "Forgive my boldness. Dinner awaits."

Angelique, nodding to hide the disappointment evident on her face, accepted the other's arm silently. She reminded herself to move slowly. They had time.

Chapter Ten

The sun sank toward the horizon, sending out long fingers of golden light that seemed to play tag with the wind, which danced in lazy dips and swirls through the high meadow grasses. The clouds, white and fluffy, sailed across a perfect spring sky. Angelique sighed, stretching an arm leisurely above her head as the fat old mare snorted and snuffled through another patch of clover.

She lay on the broad, bare back of her mare, one foot dangling on either side. Her skirts were comfortably ruffled up and not only were her petticoats showing, but her knees as well. Angelique didn't care. She had dispensed with vest and shoes altogether some time ago. Her hair was a tangled mess since she'd lost one comb and magicked the other into mischievous oblivion. And if anyone had asked, she would have gladly said she'd do it again.

It was the type of day meant for nothing but daydreams. And Angelique, for perhaps the first time in her entire life, had done just that.

At her breast, she clutched a bouquet of wild flowers. A little magick had persuaded them to forego wilting for a while longer, and they were the sum total of her day's labors. After three months of learning spells and industriously busying herself with embroidery patterns, history books and riding lessons, Angelique had finally done exactly what Culdun had been urging her to do for some time — nothing. And he'd even packed her a picnic lunch.

As she lazed in the quiet sunshine, she drew the wild flowers close again, relishing their delicate sweetness. And as the scent filled her, she remembered sweetness of another kind. She shivered, recalling how, the evening before, Drew's fingers had pushed through Angelique's thick hair and lingered, if only for a moment, before slipping a comb back into place.

Then those hands had fallen to her shoulders. Drew's

slender fingers had hesitated, before slowly dipping downward to find the fragile line of collarbone and hollow at the base of her throat. She'd closed her eyes as Drew's hands moved across her heart, leaving delicate lines of fire in their wake and a lingering memory that she would turn over again and again in her mind as she had done with all the others. But then the moment was over and Drew stepped away. There were, however, a growing number of these moments, and it was Angelique's intent to encourage a great many more.

She had taken the initiative subtly, but persistently, since her rescue from the faeries' mist. And when she'd discovered that Drew had difficulty denying her small things, she vowed to use that fact to slowly work her way into Drew's very being until they were completely entwined. Angelique knew the power her own touch evoked, and the power Drew's touch awakened in her. It was a power she was unashamedly using now to wear down Drew's stubborn resistance to mere frustration. She coerced picnics, midnight races, long parlor talks, help with her hair, help in dismounting.

Angelique was, in her heart, determined to know the truth. Perhaps that sweet protector of hers was indeed a misshapen anomaly of Nature, but she did not, for a single moment, consider it possible that Drew was truly some perverted abomination. She was more than willing to accept the bonds of marriage and all they entailed. But since the night Drew had recounted the banishment by father and stepmother, and since Drew flatly refused to discuss the actual possibility of a marriage, Angelique realized Drew would never reveal that last truth. Why had Drew's love for the stepsister been so forbidden? Drew had never actually considered their own marriage a true possibility. And so Angelique had taken on the responsibility of that final step. If Drew would not tell her willingly, then Angelique would tempt and tease and tantalize until she could demand.

Angelique assumed that, if Drew knew of her plan, Drew would think it brought on by pity. If Culdun knew, he would think it stubbornness and applaud her persistence. Her mother... Angelique suspected her mother would understand this driving desire. Her mother knew what it was like to play with fire; she would only remind her daughter to be certain she knew the costs of being burned.

Angelique sat up abruptly and the old mare snorted in protest. Determination was etched into her young face. Angelique could only begin to imagine what Drew's cost in pain and despair had been. She was not about to let Drew's opportunity fade with the twilight's mists.

As the bluish haze of the twilight rose, Angelique turned the mare toward home. The stars would be out soon enough and then it would be time for dinner and another evening of Drew's company would begin. She glanced down at the flowers in her hand with delight. She planned to arrange them for the dining table. The magicked ones always seemed too formal and she wanted something less auspicious and a bit more charming tonight.

A beautiful patch of heather beside the trail caught her eye, and Angelique reined in her mare gently. The slender stalks tempted her and she slipped to the ground with eager anticipation. The tiny, dry blossoms rustled beneath her touch as she sought the special stalk or two. Wandering down the hill, she laughed at her foolish quest. It had been her annoyance at the magicked floral perfection that had sent her out gathering the wildflowers in the first place. To be so intent on finding such perfection again seemed rather contradictory.

A sharp snap split the stillness and she fell with a cry. A sudden pain lanced through her ankle and she gripped her leg to keep from jerking her foot in the snare. The gut string was thick enough to hold, thin enough to bite the skin. Angelique remembered the rabbits her brothers had snared for dinners and the graphic pictures of their bloodied limbs. She bit her lip and inched closer to the trap, giving the line as much slack as she could.

The mare whinnied from the top of the rise, pawing at the

trail in worry. Too late Angelique remembered the warnings from both Culdun and Drew. This close to the valley's borders, she should not have risked going barefoot or straying from the path.

Again her mare neighed and pawed anxiously. Even the stable horses had been better trained to stay to those trails than she. Angelique swallowed hard, fearful that the fretting mare would work herself into leaving the safety of the hilltop path. What she should do, Angelique realized, was send the animal back as a signal for help.

She glanced around, attempting to ignore the throbbing in her foot while she gathered up a handful of pebbles. She flung one at the white mare as the animal prepared to lunge downhill. The mare stopped dead in her tracks as the stone flicked her hide. "Home!" Angelique screamed, flinging another pebble and then another. "Get yourself out of here!" Mane tossing in protest, the beast rounded and took off in a canter.

With a heartfelt sigh, Angelique slumped forward and discarded the last of her small cache of stones. The squeezing pain sliced through her ankle. She winced, grimacing as she clenched her teeth. This was worse than Aloysius' strap.

She forced herself to relax and examined the contraption more carefully. The stake was driven into the ground too deeply for her fingers to reach the knotted ends, and her inexperienced fumblings only seemed to tighten the noose.

Undoubtedly there was a spell to undo the whole lot quickly enough, but this far from the palace, the "I wish" tricks would not work. She knew she was still a long way from being a competent sorceress and this was beyond her.

Common sense told her she needed to do something to keep the cord from inadvertently tightening, and then she needed to sit quietly. Glancing about, she began tearing up the stringy roots from the heather plants behind her. When the fibers were separated, she patiently began to work them in between the snare and her ankle. She concentrated, mentally blocking out the pain just as she once had blocked out Aloysius' stinging blows. The fibers edged in slowly. She was careful to always place the next on the opposite side, attempting to offset the tension and redistribute it equally. She quit when the slicing feeling ebbed into a tight throbbing, and then she felt another stab of pain, one she recognized instantly as fear.

Above the horizon, hanging low in the dimming twilight, was the white glow of a full moon.

Angelique glanced about uneasily, curbing her panic with the reminder that the hunters never came deep into the valley until well after dark.

The sun glowed distantly, lost now behind the mountains of the horizon. But Angelique could not appreciate the sunset's beauty this night. She raised her hand to her chest, as if doing so would slow her pounding heart. Her fingers brushed across something warm and round. The talisman! Drew's words came back to her like an embrace, "Through fey dreams or mountain storms, it will reach me."

Angelique pressed the locket between trembling fingers and whispered, "Drew, please. Hear me."

The metal flashed hot and then became icy cold.

Head bowed, pressed wearily to an upraised knee, Angelique waited. Her hands were folded about the small locket. Twilight had faded to a thick grayness, but the darkness had not quite descended, telling Angelique that she had not been there as long as it seemed. It *seemed* like an eternity had passed and, given the odd tick and sway of time in this valley, she supposed it may have been forever at that.

Splitting the quiet evening air, a stallion shrieked.

Angelique started. A white steed leapt from a portal that appeared out of nowhere and onto the rest of the hill. She blinked. Was she hallucinating? No, there was Drew, dismounting even before the animal's legs had brought it fully to a halt. A torch flared as the cloaked figure paused to survey the downward sweep of the hill.

"It's a snare!" Angelique called, surprised to find her voice so hoarse. "I don't know if there are others."

If Drew heard her caution, there was no sign of it. Drew crossed the distance between them in few swift strides. Sinking down at Angelique's side, Drew said, "Your foot? Has the cord cut you?" The torch stake drove into the ground, casting light in a defiant circle.

"I don't think so." Angelique watched as Drew's hands covered her cold foot and the bruised ring on her ankle. She swallowed thickly and managed, "I'm sorry. I should have been paying more attention."

A warm hand pressed her cheek for an instant, and a gentle, teasing voice said, "I guess it's too late now to remind you about boots and snares and such."

Angelique gave Drew a half-smile.

"You did well."

Angelique blinked. There was genuine respect in the other's tone.

"These roots may have saved you from a crippling." Drew pulled out a knife and began to dig up the trap stake. "You also did well not to try your magick."

At that Angelique blushed, admitting, "I didn't know anything to try. I haven't yet gotten to sewing knots, let alone these sorts."

"No," Drew corrected, "anything would have been disastrous. After three generations of hunting in our bewitched woods, these poachers have gotten quite clever. They usually have a local witch bespell their pieces against my magick. Any spell you tried would only have tightened the cord."

Angelique gasped in pain as Drew tugged the snare free, sliced the gut string and cast the stake aside. The sting worsened as the cord was unwound from its nested niche in her skin. "I know it hurts. Try to relax now. It will be better in a few minutes," her companion murmured, thumbs stroking the swollen ankle. The pain receded. The soothing magick balm lessened the chill in her skin. Feeling began to flow back into her toes and Angelique sighed, closing her eyes to savor the relief. The throbbing became a dull ache, then finally a vague stiffness.

"Lie back."

The Snare

She did so, settling on her elbows and stretching her leg out obediently. The tender touch loosened the tautness of ankle and calf, easing the last of the cramps away. As Drew's fingers kneaded, her skin warmed and Angelique tipped her head back with a luxurious moan as the touch ascended to the sensitive place behind her knee.

Drew's hands stilled, Angelique's knee still captured in their enfolding grasp.

Angelique lifted her head. Her tousled, brown hair framed her flushed face. Her blouse had slipped from one shoulder and she could feel the intensity of Drew's gaze upon her. The flaming torch-light flickered. The shadowy depths within that crimson cloak rippled faintly.

"I want to see you, Drew."

A strangled oath squashed the flame. The torch disappeared.

As soon as they had left her lips, Angelique knew the words had been wrong. It was too soon. Cursing herself, Angelique fell silent. Drew lifted her carefully, but there was a rough, controlled anger to the movement. Then they were on the horse and Drew's booted heels were kicking them into a cantor. Drew raised a hand to call up a portal but Angelique caught it and pulled it toward her with something akin to panic.

The horse slowed to a walk. The stillness in the figure behind her chilled Angelique, but she refused to release Drew's wrist. She moistened her lips and, with her voice shaking, said, "I want to ride back with you, not jump through magick doorways."

"Why?" The voice was hard-edged, impatient.

"Because there are some pieces of your magick that still frighten me." Not a complete lie.

"Meaning I have frightened you," Drew admitted softly. There was a long pause, until Drew carefully pulled Angelique close. "My anger frightens you."

It was Angelique's turn to stiffen. She thought she might bluff her way past this moment, but stopped. She said nothing. How long had Drew known how anger frightened her? How another's rage could turn her into stone, despite her best intentions or most powerful desires? How could Drew know this one thing about her that she kept hidden from everyone?

"Even at my angriest, I have never intended to harm you," Drew's soft voice assured her, seeming to ignore her silence. "But perhaps the tenderness of a touch will reassure you where words cannot?"

Angelique's throat tightened. But Drew's hand was gentle as it brushed her thick hair aside. And Drew's breath was warm as it touched her ear. "Is this what I should do to make you believe in me?"

The kiss that pressed to her neck dissolved her fears. Lips of warmest silk kissed a slow trail to her ear, and Angelique trembled, losing herself in the delicate ecstasy of the touch. Suddenly, she didn't care what Drew knew of her heart or secret fears. This was what mattered – Drew's arms about her, the tender kisses, the soft caress.

And then suddenly, magickally, they were in the whitewashed coolness of the stables. Angelique felt the pain of betrayal with a jolt. Drew's attentions had been merely to distract her – she flushed at her own naiveté.

They dismounted. The stable master took the stallion's lead, pausing to speak with Drew about the poachers' raid that everyone was anticipating. Angelique edged away from the pair to the dividing wall between an empty stall and the tack room. Her anger melted into chagrin. Of course, Drew was never going to be fooled by any of Angelique's ploys for time or attention. Doubtless over the years her companion had often seen the game played by bolder and more curious maids than she.

But it did not explain Drew's tolerance. Curious, Angelique glanced back over her shoulder. No, there was only one possible reason Drew could have so willingly followed Angelique's coy little games. Drew wanted to be led – to be pushed. Drew would never make the first move, but would gauge a response by what stimulus had been given, and so would take as much as Angelique could bear to give. But up until recently, Drew clearly had not believed that Angelique wanted to give *everything*. And, Angelique admitted, she hadn't known it herself.

Drew turned as the stallion was led away. The stables rang momentarily with the clang of hooves on the stone floor, and then they were alone. Angelique's gaze faltered. She stared at the half-wall in front of her, a finger toying with a crack in the wooden planking. Drew approached, hesitated, and came near. From the corner of her eye, Angelique saw a hand lift to touch her and then drop.

"Have I insulted you, my Lady?"

Her hair swirled as her head shook, and she sighed breathlessly, "Do you mean by tricking me into jumping through the magick portal?"

"No."

"Then how, my Liege?"

"By holding you."

Angelique licked her lips nervously. "By holding me how?"

"Like this." Drew's arms slipped around Angelique from behind, encircling her waist and drawing her back into the thick folds of the cloak, pressing her against the warmth of Drew's stomach and long legs.

"No, not by holding me, my Liege," Angelique breathed, moving willingly, easily into Drew's embrace. She tipped her head back, baring her neck, and said in a voice edged with sweet challenge, "How else might you have given insult?"

"By kissing you?" Drew's voice was hard-edged, but this time not with anger. Angelique felt Drew's lips against her neck and she melted into the exquisite softness of endless, gentle kisses. Drew's hands, fingers spread wide, cupped the rich roundness of Angelique's breasts. Angelique let out a gasp that turned into a low, quivering moan.

Her hands folded atop Drew's as, unquestioning, she urged the heated touch higher. Drew's mouth was etching a fine line of desire across Angelique's bare shoulder, and a soft cheek brushed her skin. Her breasts ached with a tautness she had never known, and Angelique cried out, startled by the pleasure that shot through her as Drew's thumb grazed over fabric and then slid beneath the loosened bodice, palm and fingers brushing across tender skin. Angelique's knees were melting to boneless water as the lightest tip of Drew's tongue swirled about the curve of her ear.

Angelique reached a hand back, seeking support as her legs grew frighteningly weak. She clutched at Drew's shoulder and the crimson cowl pulled suddenly away.

"No."

The tenderness left their embrace. Angelique found her arms pinned against her sides, her breasts aching; the bare skin of her shoulder felt naked and chilled.

None too gently she was pushed away.

Angelique clutched at the stall's half-wall, already crying as she waited for the inevitable conclusion to this scene. It was as she'd expected. Without a word, she was left alone with her tears.

Chapter Eleven

The night was a long one for Angelique. It didn't help that the thunderstorms were raging again, or that Angelique was all too aware of Drew's departure to hunt the poachers. And though dawn brought a crystal-blue clarity to the sky above and tendrils of curling mists to the fields below, to Angelique the mist seemed eerie and only made her shiver. She paused at her terrace doors, wishing for some sign of Drew's safe return.

She should have known better than to fret. Culdun would have brought word if something dreadful had happened. With the sunrise, she knew, Drew would only have just begun the weary process of unearthing the snares and steel traps.

All the same, Angelique couldn't seem to help herself. She was dressed before the stable boys stumbled in from the village. She had nearly scrubbed the wax from the library's floor with her pacing before the sun had cleared the trees or the morning mists had begun to thin. And as she wandered the upper portico's hallways, she wondered if she hadn't somehow missed Drew's return after all. But the study was empty, as was the bed chamber. She was left to her wanderings.

She refused to think about Drew's rejection of her in the stables. She clung only to the memory of what *had* happened and to the feelings she had discovered within herself. Angelique remembered the first night in the carriage and her dreams of snakes and the deep, dark void at the end of the road. Now, the darkness no longer evoked doubts and fears. Somehow, over the last few months, she had stopped regarding the possibility of this marriage as a duty for her mother's welfare or as a necessary sacrifice for Drew's well-being. Somewhere along the way, she had come to love this extraordinary, mysterious person, and she had come to want this marriage for much more selfish reasons.

A pair of brown speckled doves cooed and nudged at one another, drawing Angelique's attention to where they sat on the stone banister. She paused, sinking soundlessly back into the shadows behind an arched column so as not to frighten them. The breeze ruffled the birds' feathers and carried with it the fresh, clean scents of the sprawling palace gardens. The upper limbs of the poplar trees that surrounded the courtyard swayed a bit. The laughter of children and the clop of a shod horse echoed across the cobblestones below, and Angelique smiled as she glanced down to see a half-dozen of the village youngsters clamoring about the rider and horse.

Poor old thing, Angelique thought, recognizing Drew's white steed as it stepped ever so cautiously about the dancing menagerie. The rider held him under a tight rein as all around them children ran, laughing and playing with the billowing length of a stolen red cloak.

It took a full moment for Angelique to realize who the slender figure upon the horse must be. Even when she did, it was first because of the rich, soft timbre to the laughter, and second because of the crimson garment that fluttered out behind the youngest child like an errant kite.

Angelique blinked in astonishment. The rider's unruly, black hair was tied back, but no longer hidden. The sculpted plains of the woman's face seemed haunted; the pallor of heart-wearied despair made her skin almost translucent in the morning sun. But Angelique also saw the soft edges of that mouth lift in laughter with the children's games. The shapeliness of the bodice, too, was no longer concealed by the hanging drape of the cloak, and Angelique suddenly remembered how soft the cheek against her shoulder had been last night.

Culdun appeared silently below, and Angelique moved quickly back from the banister as she heard her name waft up with the wind. She risked another glance. Drew was dismounting. The children had returned the cloak, and the crimson fabric was once again in place. Angelique realized Culdun must have mentioned that she was awake much earlier than usual. She returned to the depths of the hallways, trying to reconcile the haunted beauty of the woman she had just seen with Drew's description of her own monstrosity.

Her thoughts opened a gate in her mind, and Angelique

was suddenly flooded with memories and images from her childhood. Ivan's sneered remarks about a particular kitchen maid who seemed to want no man's company; her maternal grandmother's companion and the way her mother had treated them with all the respect she would have given any married couple — even in the face of Aloysius' puzzled stare and rude remarks, made when he thought no one else could hear him. She remembered other incidents, too: the taunting of a local dairymaid who, separated from her companions, was accosted at the trader's; ugly words and rumors shared on street corners and around family tables. Angelique had never paid much attention to such remarks, as it seemed her father and brothers were always mocking someone, but now, when she replaced some of those other tormented and shamed faces with Drew's, she began to understand the depth of Drew's despair and why Drew had come to see herself as the monstrous outcast. An outcast who simply *must* have deserved a father's wrath and a stepmother's curse.

But Angelique did not believe people like the witch-woman or Aloysius were right in their opinions. As a matter of course, Angelique reminded herself, she'd generally found that those who held opinions in opposition to hers were usually the ones whose hearts were corrupted by greed — just like Aloysius or Drew's stepmother. How could Drew's father not have seen the blatant lies inherent in the discovery of the so-called atrocity which Drew was to have perpetuated?! Suddenly, Angelique felt a hot flame of pure rage kindle within her — whatever atrocities that witch-woman had named Drew, the naming had been the atrocity, not Drew!

And as for Drew herself, well, no matter what Drew had encountered in the other maids before Angelique, how dare she assume Angelique was as simple-minded!

"Culdun!" she called, her voice ringing with determination. Still crying his name, she spun on her heel and headed for the nearest stairwell.

The time for foolishness was done.

Chapter Twelve

"What do you mean, not coming?" Angelique gasped. "My Liege has retired without breakfast, Mistress. There were poachers about last night."

"I'm quite aware of what transpired last night, Culdun. Just as you are quite aware of the fact that we brunch together on such days *before* Drew goes off to bed. So tell me. What is going on?"

The Old One stared at her for a long while. Quietly he said, "Perhaps you should be telling me."

Angelique's mouth thinned, her dark eyes smoldering with gathering fury. "I don't know what you mean. All I know is that Drew is running away again!" Angelique hissed, catching Culdun completely by surprise. "And *you* are helping her to do it!"

His face went blank. But not before Angelique glimpsed his surprise and shock. There was a tense silence. "I saw Drew this morning from the balcony," she paused and then added, "without the hood. I saw *her*, Culdun. What she's been trying to hide from me all this time."

"Does my Liege know?"

"No. And you are not to say one single word about it, either. This is for us to work out alone. But damn it, Culdun! It's so hard when she won't even meet me half-way!"

The Old One offered a sad smile. "I would imagine not. There has been so much pain and many, many years of loneliness, my Lady."

"Culdun, will you help her hide forever?"

Culdun gave her a measured look and Angelique could seem him weighing the respect he felt for her against the oaths he'd sworn to his Liege. With a nod, he consented. "My Liege requested tea in the private gardens at four."

"The secluded one? The place her study windows overlook?"

He nodded.

"How do I gain entrance, Culdun? I know there is no usual path."

"Aye, my Lady. But I can show you."

The water sparkled in the fountain like a splay of diamond dust. Angelique dipped her fingers into the cool pool and sighed. Drew was late. She worried the woman may have come and gone, slipping away unseen when she caught sight of Angelique waiting for her.

"Will you wait a while longer, my Lady?" China rattled as Culdun arranged the tea service on the little white table.

Angelique nodded morosely.

"My Lady?"

Angelique glanced up to find Culdun poised with the tea pot and a cup in hand. She shook her head. "Nothing right now, Culdun. Thank you."

He set the cup and pot back on the table and rummaged in his pockets for a moment. "Ah, I'd almost forgotten," he said, drawing out a rolled parchment. "This arrived this morning. It's from your mother."

"Thank you." She accepted the bundle, which was tied with a red ribbon, and wondered vaguely if Aloysius had finally found a nursing companion who could write. The letter was quite a bit thicker than her father's patience generally allowed.

Culdun's broad hand touched hers gently. "You will do fine."

"Yes," she gave him a wan smile. "Thank you. Please, don't let me keep you from your work. With this heat your garden must need tending."

"But I'll still be near." He gave her hand an encouraging squeeze and departed.

The fountain's babbling blended with the birds' chatter. But Angelique was barely aware of her surroundings. With a determined shake of her head, she broke the wax seal of her mother's letter.

She found she'd been correct in her assumptions; Aloysius had hired an educated nurse to oversee her mother's care. Angelique thought how very well things must be going for her father with Drew's wares. Again she shook her head. She would not let his memory spoil the pleasure of a letter from her mother. Focusing on that, she began to read and, as she did, could almost hear her mother's loving voice describing the long quiet days.

The breeze died unnoticed. The chirp and peep of the birds dwindled, then quieted altogether. Only the sound of the running water in the fountain behind her persisted, and gradually, Angelique became aware of the stillness. She looked up slowly, knowing already she was not alone. Between the straight columns, half-cloaked by the shadows of the palace archways, Drew stood silently.

Angelique offered a smile and went back to her reading. She could no more concentrate on the words in front of her than she could quiet the pounding beat of her heart. But she was wary of startling Drew again. Something deep within Angelique had finally grasped how very thin Drew's façade of strength was, and Angelique wanted nothing more than to offer protection to the frightened child hidden behind all that false bravado.

"A letter from home, my Lady?"

In relief, Angelique breathed again.

"Yes." She lifted a welcoming gaze as the hooded Drew neared. "It's from Mama. She writes that Aloysius has come down with his usual summer cold even though the house has never been warmer. Since his business is thriving, he apparently has all the hearths burning night and day."

"I am glad they are doing well for your mother's sake."

Angelique's smile faltered as she watched black-gloved hands move from her sight.

"I am sorry I am late for tea." Drew offered a small bow. "I did not expect your company."

"You must be hungry." Angelique stood. A magickal command whisked the letter off to her bed chambers, and she moved to the table. "Would you like sugar or honey?"

"Honey, thank you."

The lid to the silver pot rattled and threatened to slip. Angelique set it down with a betraying bump. The cups clattered with the jolt.

"Are you alright? Angelique?"

She turned at the concern in the voice, leaning back to grasp the edges of the table, and admitted honestly, "Only nervous, my Liege."

A half-step drew the other forward, and then that hesitant pose emerged. "I must apologize for last night, my Lady. I —"

"Drew." Angelique's voice was breathless with anxiety. A palpable tension hung in the air between them. "I want you to promise me something."

"That would depend on what it is you ask."

"Promise me that you won't run away today."

Startled, Drew took a step backward. "I am not sure I can give you such a promise," she said quietly.

"I just want to talk with you, Drew. There are things I need to say. Will you hear me out, at least?"

"Do I listen so poorly, my Lady?"

"Sometimes," Angelique admitted, refusing to extend a false reassurance even though her heart so much wanted to. "Sometimes you only hear the part that reinforces what you are so certain is true, and nothing else. I need you to listen to everything, Drew. To really listen."

"I will do my best. You have my promise on that."

"And you will stay? No matter what?" Angelique pressed.

"You have my word, Angelique."

"I want more than your word, Drew. I want you."

"I am here. Say what you have to say."

Angelique sighed. Already Drew was not listening. Angelique stepped forward, offering her hands. Drew grasped them obediently, and Angelique pulled them close to her breast, holding them tightly in defiance of escape. She glanced down at the black leather gloves. "I thought we were done with these. Why have you put them on again?"

Drew hesitated. "I dare not risk —"

"What?" Angelique challenged softly, her eyes searching

the dark void. "The feelings that you awaken in me when your hands touch my skin? The feelings the touch awakens in you? Simply because ignorant people believe that one woman should not touch another woman in love?"

Drew started and began to pull away, but Angelique held tight to her hands. "No. Listen to me, Drew. You promised to listen to me. I know you are a woman. I saw you ride in with the children this morning. I know your skin has a pallor that cries out for the kiss of the sun and a softness that cries for a woman's touch. I've seen your hair lift in the breeze. Why do you hide it under that terrible cloak? I know the shape of you now, Drew. The curves the cloak hides. I know you are a woman, Drew. But what I don't know is why I should fear you. Where is this abomination you spoke of? I saw nothing but a beautiful woman too long denied everything."

Drew pulled away sharply. Turning her back, she reached up to cover her face with her hands. Angelique moved swiftly toward her, but stopped short of embracing that taut figure from behind. "Drew," Angelique whispered. "You are beautiful. There is nothing horrible about you. Please, don't deny me any longer."

There was no answer. There was no movement. Slowly, Drew lifted the cloak from her head and let it fall to the ground. She pulled the gloves off unhurriedly. Like shadows melting with the rising sun or smoke blown from a fire, the cloak and gloves disappeared.

The breath caught in Angelique's throat as the taller woman turned. The darkest sable-hued eyes she'd ever seen stared at her, so full of fear that Angelique felt her heart would burst. She longed to smooth the knotted brow, ease away the years of self-hatred and doubt. Moving closer, she raised a tentative hand and brushed a tendril of ebony hair aside, letting her fingers linger on its silky softness. Her fingers slipped beneath its satin weight to cup the nape of Drew's neck. Tugging gently, she pulled Drew's mouth toward hers.

"This is wrong," Drew protested fearfully. "It will damn you to hell."

"No," Angelique murmured. "It was your stepmother who

was sent to hell for her hatred and greed. You are not damned, beloved. And neither am I."

Angelique kissed her, pressing her lips softly and tenderly against Drew's. The other woman did not respond at first, but Angelique persisted until she felt Drew begin to relax into the kiss. A flood of desire opened within her and she pressed against Drew, remembering a thousand casual and not so casual touches, the feeling of Drew's fingertips on her skin, the tender mouth against her shoulder. She pulled back reluctantly as Drew broke the kiss to find tears streaming down Drew's face.

"I hope those are tears of happiness," Angelique said softly as her hands cradled the warm, wet cheeks.

But a sob caught in Drew's throat, and she pulled away. Helplessly, Drew shook her head. "I can't. Not with you."

"Only with me," Angelique corrected swiftly.

"No —"

"— but you love me!" Angelique protested. "I know you do!"

"*Because* I do...."

Drawing a short breath, Angelique bit her tongue hard to stop the retort. She thought for a long moment, waiting while Drew gathered herself together. "Does it make any difference that I love you, too?"

"You cannot."

Angelique glared at her, warning, "Don't tell me who I can or cannot love, Drew. I am the mistress of my own heart and I have given it to you."

Panic flashed across Drew's face. "Please," she said. "Don't. You will only be disappointed."

Angelique shook her head. "I will not be disappointed in you, beloved. But I understand. I cannot expect one kiss to erase lifetimes of pain. It is unreasonable of me to expect you to forget all those empty years in one instant. But I am patient, Drew. And you will not be rid of me so easily. In fact," she added, "try as you might, you cannot get rid of me at all. You said this is my home, Drew. And I intend to hold you to your word."

Drew said nothing and her face was a careful blank. But

Angelique was not dissuaded. "Now," she said lightly, "sit down and have your tea."

Chapter Thirteen

A bird sang somewhere, and Angelique stirred, sighing blissfully at the warm sun on her face. A light touch brushed a lock of hair from her forehead. She turned her cheek into the soft fabric, half asleep in Drew's lap.

"We should be thinking of going," Drew sighed, but there was no real urgency in her voice.

Angelique opened her eyes and stared up into the cautious, yet hopeful, face of her companion. As their eyes met, Angelique felt desire rise within her and felt, as though it were a tangible thing, the same feelings spark in Drew. Drew leaned over Angelique, kissed her gently, and then pulled away reluctantly. She still feared where giving herself permission to touch Angelique would lead them. "Perhaps this was not such a good idea after all," Drew managed, swallowing hard against the hoarseness of her voice.

"Yes, it was and you know it. You needed the time away from your star charts and calendars."

"The work is necessary –"

"But one cannot work all the time, my Liege."

Drew looked off to the horizon of sun and mountains and the tension slowly eased in her body.

"What are you thinking?" Angelique asked.

The question drew a chuckle from the other.

"Tell me, please?"

"I was thinking that you are right," Drew allowed, glancing down at her. "This was a good idea. It has been a good day for me, despite myself and all my initial reservations."

"A good day for *us*," Angelique corrected, lifting Drew's hand to weave their fingers together.

"For us." Drew looked upward again, her eyes following the lines and contours of the valley around them. "There is so much here I have always taken for granted. I believe you may have begun to show me how precious this place can really be."

"Everyone should know the feeling of a true home," Angelique murmured, but her voice trailed off as she remembered the letter she'd received last evening.

"What is it, Angelique?"

For a moment Angelique was silent, then said, "It is my mother. Thinking of how much this place has become home to me reminded me that Aloysius' house has never truly been a home for her. And now she seems worse."

"Did the letter say that?"

Angelique shook her head. "Not so boldly, but it was very short for Mama. She has so little to do save dictate these letters, yet it was merely a note. That worries me."

Drew sighed. "I wish I could bring her here for you. I wish she was strong enough for the journey."

"I know she is not," Angelique admitted. "If I simply sat beside her and moved quickly, the pain she felt was excruciating. She would never survive a carriage ride."

"And my magick cannot summon her unless she already belongs to this place. That limit is part of the spell that binds me here," her companion noted.

"I know," Angelique whispered, sitting up and wrapping her arms around Drew's shoulders. "She cannot whisk here and back as Culdun and the caravans do."

"Sometimes I think my stepmother must have feared me more than I knew."

"Feared that you would pull her into this limbo with you?" Angelique let her arms fall and she took Drew's hands in her own.

"Not her, perhaps. Her daughter."

"Did you want to? Did you try?"

Drew shook her head. "She would have had to come here freely. For a long time I hoped that she would somehow choose to. But time passed and I grew wiser. She is dead now of old age, Angelique. She has long been dust."

"Did you love her that much?" Angelique breathed, caught between compassion and jealousy, even though she knew she had no real cause to be jealous.

"I thought I did. Once." Drew pulled listlessly at the

grass beside her. "But that was a foolish dream."

"You were young. Do not be so hard on yourself."

The muscles in Drew's jaw jumped. "How can I not be? I was banished for her sake! Duped into thinking she loved me. How could I have been such a fool? How could I not have seen that she didn't care for me? Couldn't love me? How can anyone–" She broke off and shook her head.

"What, Drew? Love you?"

Drew closed her eyes and said nothing.

Angelique turned Drew's face toward her with one gentle hand. "What will it take to convince you that I am not like the others? That I do love you, despite your imaginings that it is otherwise?"

"But don't you want something more? A family? Children of your own? Loving me will only court your damnation."

Angelique shook her head. "Enough of that. It's ridiculous. Your stepmother twisted religion and myth to her whim. If you know nothing else, Drew, know that I would not choose a life like my mother's for anything in this world. A life worn thin with a husband's demands, bearing child after child, biting my tongue and suppressing my opinion until I believed I never had one. Only in the end to be forsaken by lover and husband, worn through by years of incredible physical pain that no tincture can ease. Her disease of the bones is inherited, you know. At least here, when the pain grows too severe, I can walk into the faeries' mist and be rid of it forever."

Horror flickered in Drew's dark eyes. "You cannot know for certain that this disease will strike you!"

"Nothing is certain, no. But my aunt suffered the same ailments. There is the risk. But with you I would not be forsaken. And neither will I be damned."

"If you choose, I could bind you into youth. Then that pain would never touch you at all. If you stay–"

"And wed you?"

Drew hesitated and did not answer.

"So, you would ask me to stay and watch as another maid comes to break your curse and my heart in the process?"

"There will not be another." Angelique studied Drew's tense, closed face. Darkness churned in the depths of her eyes as she repeated, "There will never be another."

A small glow lit in the corner of Angelique's heart. "Not even a faery maid?"

Drew's eyes flashed surprise at Angelique's perceptive guess. "Not even a faery maid."

"Have I your word, my Liege?" Angelique's voice was touched with possessive mischief.

Drew bowed her head. "You have my word, my Lady."

Their eyes met for a moment as Drew admitted with a grin, "Even the lure of the faery lands grows thin after a time, especially if you do not succumb to the wines. Faery maidens have no real attachments except for their music. Nor does their touch break the curse."

"That is just as well," Angelique assured her, sliding an arm into Drew's and dragging her off toward their tethered horses. "Married or not, my Liege, your dancing eves are done unless I'm included!"

Days drifted into weeks as Angelique found her beloved's resistance slowly ebbing, and their habits began to settle into routines. She seldom spent the mornings with Drew, but with Culdun's aid she had begun an experiment with a new sort of garden that was a mixture of wild and domesticated plants, and it consumed a good deal of Angelique's energies. Afternoons, however, brought Drew to her, and they shared the more leisurely affairs of picnics in hidden meadows or rides through the cool forest. Angelique found herself growing into something of a philosopher, as well, an interest Drew encouraged, and often tea was accompanied by animated discussions. The questions raised nearly always spurred Angelique back to the libraries before dinner.

Her magickal skills continued to grow, but Angelique was still very much aware of her limits. She was largely reliant on the magickal energies of her environment and found out early that a trick easily done in the palace worked less well in the forest, despite the presence of the faery magick and the accompanying mist. That fey magick had nurtured the trees, and so she was certainly a better sorceress in the woods than out on the meadows or in the fields, but she was sometimes still frustrated with her limitations. Drew only smiled and encouraged her to persist, reminding Angelique that it had taken her years to move beyond the arcane restrictions Angelique was just now encountering.

Despite this, however, Angelique took a quiet joy in magick, particularly the smaller sorts such as the ability to place a comb in her hair and command it to stay, the murmured word that adjusted the temperature of the bath water to the perfect degree, or the spell that caused the fountain pool to reflect Culdun's whereabouts. These were the talents Angelique found the most rewarding.

And it was the reflecting spell that dominated their conversation one evening as they dawdled over a half-finished game of backgammon. "Despite what it seems, that is not a simple spell. There is more to it."

"I thought there must be!" Angelique exclaimed. "I stumbled upon it in one of your older books, the ones bound in red leather. I tried for an hour before I could get the pool to show me Culdun, and then only if he were on the palace grounds. It wouldn't show me you at all."

"No, it wouldn't have. I am another magickian. You would need to tailor it very precisely to find anyone else versed in the magickal arts."

"Whereas Culdun is not so versed?"

An easy smile came to her companion, bringing a touch of youth with it. "Not as you and I know magick, my Lady. The Old Ones work with the earth and with the netherworld. They are part of everything and everything is part of them. The only real spells you have seen Culdun do are palace magick – the spells which answer to 'I wish' or 'I need.'"

"But I've seen him simply appear from nowhere. I've seen him do it between the village and the gardens as well."

"Ah, but that is different. He does not use the portals as I do. Between here and the village, he steps into the faeries' mist. Time does not exist in a forward motion there. It is much more convoluted. He understands those currents and eddies even better than I do and uses them to hurry between places in the valley when he has need. He and the others travel there with my talismans and beneath my protection."

"Then the reflection spell lets me find him because he's not warded against it. Whereas you are."

"Yes," Drew nodded, pleased at Angelique's insight. "Early in my exile, I took the precaution of guarding myself against any secret observations. Initially, I worried my stepmother would return to wreak more havoc, especially if her daughter were truly as marred by my so-called abuse as she'd claimed. Later it was useful in avoiding the clumsier enchantments of the occasional witch hired by the poachers."

"And now you hide from me as well?"

"Actually, I seem rather incapable of that," Drew admitted with a wry smile.

"Can you teach me?"

"Although I can guide you, Angelique, I cannot actually teach you magick, for it is a personal thing to be learned alone. But I can tell you that when I was first studying, I kept a journal. You will find it among the loose parchments in the black leather folders."

"The ones in your study?"

"Yes. You will find help with the reflection spell. And much more. They will warn against the more common, awkward mistakes."

"Do they address the seeking of another sorceress?"

"No." Drew sat back with a faint shake of her head. "Wards are intensely personalized to each spell caster. Although you will be able to use the same basic knowledge to help you, they must each be broken differently."

"Oh."

"But the notes do address some of the other matters which concern you, such as greater distances," Drew encouraged. "When you are adept enough to find Culdun or his nieces in the village, you should also be able to see your mother back home."

"That would be wonderful," Angelique admitted. "But I wish you would quit referring to Aloysius' house as my home. This is my home, Drew. In this place. With you."

It took longer for the haunted shadow to appear this time, and Angelique noticed the brief moment of pleasure which lit Drew's eyes before the doubt closed in again. She rose and rounded the small table, smiling with fond amusement as Drew's chair scraped in her haste to rise politely.

"I am going to bed now," Angelique announced, calmly, looking up into those pensive eyes. "I intend to dream wonderful dreams of magick and love. I know that look on your face, my Liege. And I refuse to stay and allow you to torment us both with all that noble nonsense about not marrying me." Drew opened her mouth to protest, but Angelique lay a slender finger against the other woman's lips and said, "I will hear no argument from you tonight. Now, give me my good-night kiss."

Drew bent, brushing her lips across Angelique's. Angelique sighed happily, brown eyes shining as Drew straightened. Unexpectedly, Drew pulled Angelique close and kissed her again, much less cautiously this time.

The sheer possessiveness of it stole Angelique's breath. Desire parted her lips, and she moaned as she felt Drew respond in kind. The kiss deepened, and Drew slipped her hand under Angelique's thick hair to cup the nape of her neck. The world spun as Angelique lost herself in the sudden, surging rise of desire.

Drew pulled back very slowly, but she did not release Angelique when she paused once more to draw breath. One hand was still buried in Angelique's hair; the other cupped her cheek. Angelique gazed up into the unreadable depths of Drew's gaze as she waited for the other to speak.

Angelique expected another denial of the love they shared, but instead was rewarded. Drew whispered, "With each passing day it seems..." she faltered. Angelique held her breath. For a moment she thought Drew would simply shake her head and take her leave, but Drew took a slow breath and continued,

"It seems more possible."

Angelique did not have to ask what seemed possible. There could only be one response. A tentative smile of encouragement played about her lips as Angelique replied, "Each time you hold me, I find myself praying this will be the time you will not let go."

Drew's eyes narrowed and her smile became a little strained. But she did not move away. For a long moment, they stood together, held in a kind of limbo, an unspoken question between them. It was Drew who shifted first. She bent again to kiss Angelique, but this time it was almost chaste.

"But this is not the time. Is it, my Liege?"

Drew shook her head. She lifted her hands to hold Angelique's face between them. "Will you wait for me, Angelique? Can I beg yet a little more of your patience?"

"For you, my love, I would wait forever."

Chapter Fourteen

The summer air was thick with the scent of roses. The fountain sang and a pair of wrens fluttered and fluffed in the shallow waters, adding their cheerful squabbling to the afternoon.

But the tea had grown cold on the little white table, and Angelique was mournfully dangling a hand in the fountain pool. Her thick hair was pulled back by only a single comb, one side left free to hang as its hairpiece lay forgotten beside her. The soft lines of her face were marred by a faint frown.

"I have never seen you quite so unhappy," Drew murmured, appearing from one of her magickal portals. "I am sorry I am so late. I did not mean to upset you."

"You haven't." Angelique withdrew her hand from the water, shaking the droplets free. "You said you would be delayed." She retrieved the comb and set about fixing her hair. "Are you ready for tea?" Angelique rose and, with a few words, warmed the pot again. "There is soft cheese and black bread as well. Or if you would prefer–"

"That will be fine," Drew broke in. She settled at the table, watching Angelique pour the tea. After a moment she asked, "Have I done something to offend you, my Lady? Or forgotten something? I know it is not your birthday, but perhaps your mother's?"

"No. It's not that." She smiled wryly and looked at Drew. "It is not a birthday. It is a wedding day."

"Yes," Drew began cautiously, "Culdun's niece. It—" She broke off as sudden understanding dawned in her dark eyes, and looked away. "You are unhappy because it is not *our* wedding day." She paused and then added dismally, "Whatever I do, I seem bound to hurt you."

"You do not hurt me on purpose, Drew. I understand your fears. But, sometimes, that doesn't make the hurt any less." Angelique raised her eyes to Drew's face, her disappointment plain. But when she saw the pain her own words had caused, she regretted her selfishness. "Now I've hurt you. Oh, Drew, I don't seem to be able to do anything right today."

"The tea is good," the other offered with a shy smile.

"Can you forgive me?"

"Of course." Drew brightened. "Not only can I forgive you, but I can also at least try to lift your melancholy. Let me escort you to the wedding feast? It would be an honor to have you on my arm."

Angelique came around the table and answered her question with a kiss.

The wedding was more a village celebration than a ceremony, and Angelique was glad she had not missed it. Everyone was there, even babes too young to walk, held by fathers and mothers throughout the gleeful dancing. Elders and youths shared tankards of ale together, spun tales, and ate with great gusto at many of the heavily-laden tables of food.

Angelique settled down at the edge of the festivities. She'd lost sight of Drew some time ago now amid the shouted greetings. Drew, it seemed, was a popular dancing partner and had been whisked away even before Angelique had been able to protest. She scanned the crowd, but of Drew she saw no sign.

"I see you've found yourself a safe place to watch all the going on."

"I feel so out of place here, Culdun!" Angelique admitted with a grin, as the small man slid onto the bench next to her.

"You? Don't be silly. You look like you were born here!"

She laughed. She was taller than his folk by more than a head and clumsy as a drunken bear compared to the willowy faery folk.

"Nay, wave me off like some shallow youth," he snorted, then finished his drink.

Angelique's brows lifted, a thought dawning as she peered at him more closely.

"Your dress, my Lady, is what I'm referring to. Colors of autumn bright – harvest bright." He waved to the dancers. The faery folk jumped the bonfire, slivers of twilight dust scattering with the orange sparks as they cleared the flames' summit. "Just like any of us."

"Culdun."

Obediently, he turned huge, gray eyes toward her.

"You're drunk."

A shout of laughter and a hand clasped her knee as he rocked in his seat, almost slipping to the ground, but he didn't seem in the least concerned. He wiped the tears from his eyes and, still gurgling a bit, answered, "You're right there. But that's what a wedding's for, mistress." Culdun paused, and added carefully, "Sure you won't have a taste?" He waved back at the dancers.

Angelique almost laughed again and shook her head, but then she registered the serious note in his question. She looked out. The crowd had stilled their feet, their hands clapping in time to the drummer's beat. In the center of the ring, a youth was on his knees and leaning back, a slender torch held high. The gold and amber of the flame matched the colors of his clothing. His hair was as bright as the flame of the setting sun. The crowd laughed and spurred him on as he bent back further until his head nearly touched the ground behind. Then suddenly the flame disappeared as he swallowed the whole of its fiery ball.

With a shout of triumph he discarded the stick. Applause and cheers greeted him as he sprang into the air, somersaulting backwards – not once, but twice. On the third hop and fling, though, he faltered, landing in a sprawling heap amidst the bare feet and tattered skirts of a village girl. The crowd chided him playfully at the obvious ploy as the maid bent beside the still form of the acrobat. He abruptly awakened and stole a kiss, and the music began again. Angelique noticed the couple leave the circle to seek out the more private depths of the forest's darkness. She looked to Culdun.

"It is a night of rashness, my Lady." Culdun lifted his bushy brows. "It is a night to forget caution, to throw the dice in a gamble or two. The maids flirt—" Culdun gestured to the dancing and Angelique now saw it was just an excuse for a touch or a glance. "The youths entreat—" Blushing, Angelique turned away. Culdun continued, "Some sample sweets with no thoughts of future feasts. Others," Culdun shrugged with deliberate casualness, "use the night's enchantment as a way to make it plain to their beloved that the time is ripe to hurry the inevitable."

"The inevitable?"

"Marriage."

Angelique nodded in response, but her thoughts were already elsewhere. Her fingers moved unconsciously to the magickal locket about her neck and didn't see Culdun hide his smile in his cup as he pretended to drain a last droplet or two.

Angelique's eyes scanned the dancers. Culdun lifted a finger and pointed across the clearing. "There, my Lady."

Her fingers dropped from the locket as she touched his shoulder gratefully. Then she left him and moved unerringly toward Drew. Culdun watched her go.

"And what are you looking so pleased about, you romantic old fool?" A stocky young man plunked down in the emptied seat and poured half of his wine into Culdun's cup. The other thanked him with a grin.

"Look at them." Culdun nodded to where Drew and Angelique stood together, their clothes highlighted by the fire's red glow.

Their faces were shadowed, and as Angelique pressed close to Drew the young man said, "You say she's the one?"

"Aye!" Culdun nodded vigorously. "The very one."

"Then we've all cause for more celebration!" The younger man wrapped an arm about Culdun's neck and they toasted together. Then the younger man pulled Culdun close for a sound kiss.

"I was wondering when you were going to get around to that." Culdun grinned when their kiss ended. Arms around each other, they staggered to their feet.

"Come along now before I throw you across these broad shoulders of mine and make a complete spectacle out of both of us!"

"No need for that," Culdun laughed and they made their way home.

"Drew, I want to dance," Angelique announced, as she pressed herself close to her beloved. "You have honored everyone but me tonight, it seems, with the pleasure of your company." Her words were light and breathless, but her eyes boldly devoured the woman before her.

Drew was truly dressed to honor the Old Ones tonight, her garb of bright autumn copper and bronze replacing her usual somber tones. She'd exchanged her white tunic for a gold-colored billowy shirt with ribbon-sliced sleeves. Her ebony hair was tied back but for the thin braid before her left ear, and her cheekbones had been painted like the other Elders' with the green diamond-headed snakes.

"Should I trust the faery folk, do you think?" Angelique waved at the musicians and dancers. "As partners, I mean?"

Concern flared in those dark eyes and Angelique was satisfied her teasing had found its mark. "Or should I bid you to come dance instead? After all, you are my escort."

Angelique's smile was contagious, her humor infectious. Drew answered with a soft laugh. Angelique gave Drew no time to change her mind but grasped her hand and pulled her along. Culdun was right; tonight was a night for gambling.

They danced until they were parched, then shared a drought of ale and a plate of cheese, bread and meat before dancing again. If Drew noticed Angelique's stumbled steps caused her to fall a bit more often into those strong arms, she gave no sign. If the cheese was suspiciously so good that Angelique was prompted to share her bite with her companion and her fingers lingered over-long along the soft line of Drew's mouth, Drew kept her own counsel.

Slowly, Angelique became aware of a tighter grasp about her waist as they spun, of the hand that tipped her chin as the stein was held for her to drink, of the burning power in that dark gaze as it began to follow her every move. And she laughed, delight mingling with excitement. Caution sizzled into oblivion as she met bold gaze with bold gaze.

It was her night, finally, to demand.

Spinning, nearly falling, Angelique dragged Drew out of the mayhem of music to the flickering edges of the firelight's reach. A tree offered her a brace and, gasping for breath, she leaned back gratefully.

Drew's fingers reached out, lifting Angelique's thick braid aside. The laces on her blouse had come loose during the dancing and Angelique felt a shiver at the night's coolness upon her skin, but she made no move to retie them. Drew's touch lingered on her bare shoulder, and she shivered for another reason. She moistened her lips as Drew moved closer, blocking the fete from sight and thought. Angelique met Drew's dark gaze for less than a heartbeat before Drew's mouth found hers.

Angelique's kiss was hungry, demanding, and Drew's arms closed fast about her, answering her need, pulling her nearer. Her toes barely touched the earth as she was lifted into Drew's embrace, and she clung to Drew's shoulders as Drew's hungry mouth forged ragged paths down the pulsing lines of her throat. She gasped and trembled. Drew moved her kisses upwards to Angelique's ear and, as she did so, Angelique's own mouth tasted Drew's tender skin. Angelique trembled again, this time at the quivering she caused in the other. Her teeth bit lightly and she groaned as her ear was touched by hot breath and teasing tongue.

Drew's voice was heated. "Lie with me tonight." It was not a question, but a statement.

"Yes!" Angelique's feet returned to the ground as they kissed again, and she repeated her fervent reply, "Please, yes!"

Drew pulled back suddenly. Before Angelique could speak, Drew said, "Not here. At home," and swept her up, carrying her into the shadows. The white stallion snorted at their arrival, calming with a murmured word. They mounted, Angelique safely gathered in her beloved's arms as the horse stepped off down the trail.

Desire flamed in Drew's dark gaze. Angelique untied the

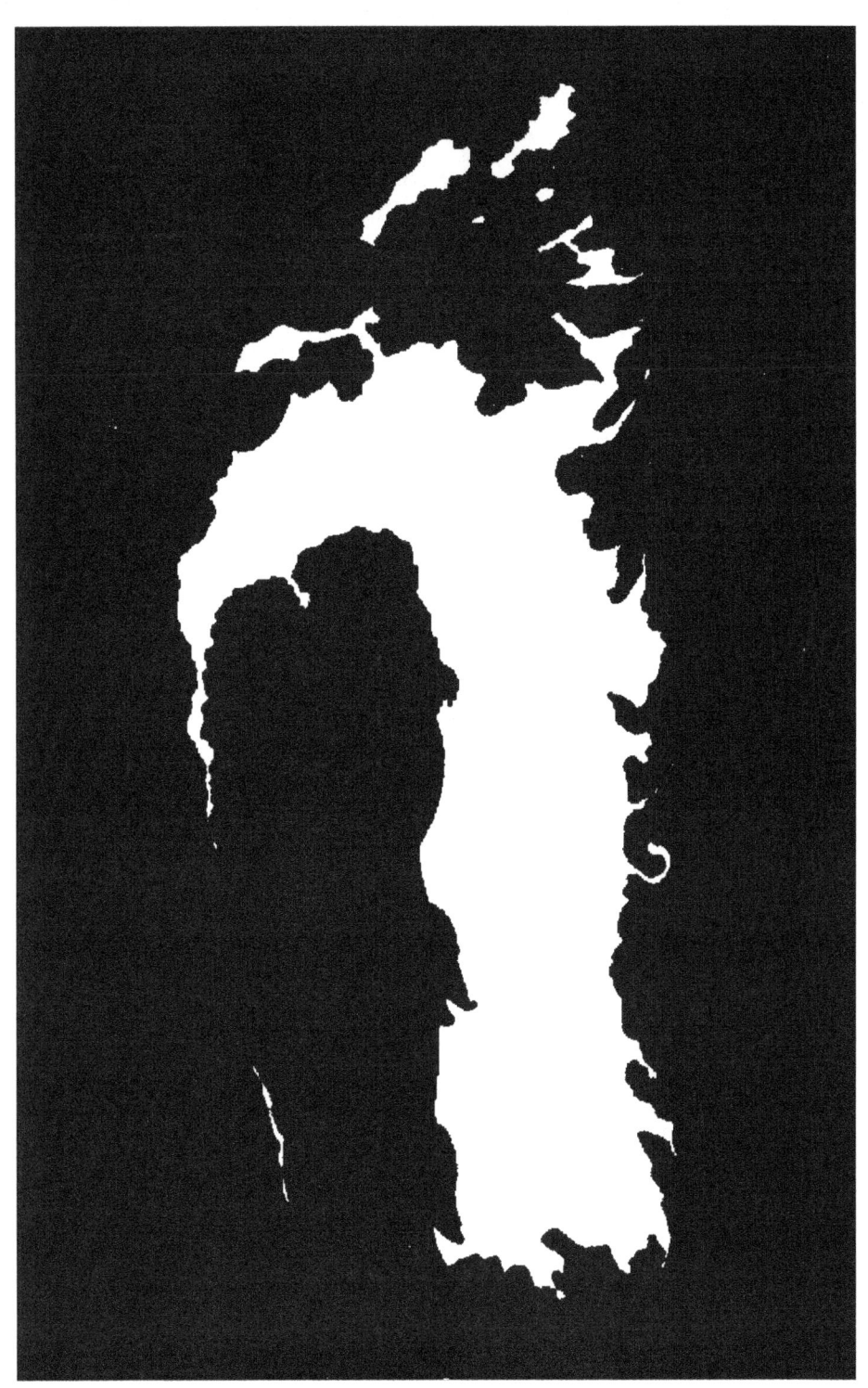

The Kiss

top lacing of Drew's vest and felt a heart thudding in racing time with her own.

The magick portal opened. They came home.

A breeze blew gently. Angelique shivered with the night's chill until Drew's voice whispered her name and she forgot the world again. Her arms slid around her beloved's neck as they dismounted before the stables, then were in Angelique's room a heartbeat later.

A fire blazed into life, brightening the dimness. The bedding turned down with a magickal flourish. Slowly, Drew set her on her feet.

Angelique returned to her unfinished task of quietly untying Drew's vest. She paused at the last knot, to answer the question on Drew's face. She smiled and answered again, "Yes."

The mouth that took hers this time was gentle and soft. She sank back into the crisp sheets and pulled Drew down on top of her. There, they paused. Angelique stared into Drew's dark eyes and, finding what she sought there, abandoned herself to the power of Drew's touch.

A gentle finger pushed the silken strands from her brow. Slowly, Angelique roused herself from sleep.

Angelique's smile deepened as Drew said, "I didn't mean to wake you."

"Don't stop." Angelique put up a hand. "It feels nice. You feel nice."

"Do you need to sleep?"

"In a bit."

An answering smile fluttered across Drew's face, and it pleased Angelique to see her beloved relax beside her. Angelique's body glowed with the sated calm left from Drew's lovemaking. The faint ache in her muscles was a tangible testimony. Lying beside Drew, Angelique felt only their love. For tonight, at least, all their ghosts were banished.

She nuzzled into Drew's fingers and sighed as the warm

palm cupped her cheek. "Thank you." The question on Drew's face prompted Angelique to add, "For the light."

"Ah." Drew glanced up. The pale blue of magickal fireflies danced lazily about the ceiling.

"A starry blanket for a lovely night," Angelique murmured. "I like being able to see you and knowing you see me."

"You never liked it when I hid from you."

Angelique touched Drew's face, turned it toward her in the light. For a moment, neither spoke. Then, "May I touch you?"

As if in answer, Drew's breath came in short, shallow gasps.

"I want my turn. To please you."

"I don't know if I can."

"You can, Drew. Let me. Please."

For a long moment, Drew hesitated, but finally, she nodded.

Unhurriedly, Angelique let her hand curl against Drew's cheek. Drew's dark eyes closed and her body arched with need, baring her throat for Angelique's kisses.

"Yes, beloved." Angelique pressed satin kisses to that pulsing line. Tension melted into desire as trust replaced fear. There would be no interruption this time. No denial. Angelique shifted, her touches growing bolder. And a shudder of another kind began within Drew as Angelique bent her head to the smooth skin that covered the gentle curve of Drew's collarbone, kissing the skin softly. Her gentle coaxing muffled, she took Drew's breast into her mouth. Drew gasped, sinking her fingers deep into Angelique's hair to pull her closer. Angelique complied.

When Drew's nipples were both hard as polished gems against her tongue, Angelique shifted, laying her head against Drew's belly, and encircled Drew's waist with her arm. Her other hand brushed across crisp curls and then her fingers sank into wetness. "Oh, so ready!" Angelique felt her own desire rise again with the homage paid her by Drew's desire.

Drew's hand found Angelique's wrist and pressed the

touch down. Angelique's fingertips glided in whirling temptation. Drew's hips lifted, offering herself to Angelique's touch. With a deep-throated "Yes," Angelique encouraged her abandon.

"Please—"

"Love—" Angelique slipped her fingers into Drew and felt her own muscles contract as Drew held her there. Drew pushed against her, and together they quickly found a rhythm that caught her lover in its whirlwind, spinning her higher as Angelique watched, held and pushed deeper for her.

"Oh yes, my love. Yes," Angelique breathed. She felt the gathering of tension in Drew's body and, with a moan, sank her mouth into Drew's wetness.

Drew arched as neither fingers nor tongue relented. With a joyous cry and sudden release, purgatory vanished and both hearts soared into heaven.

Chapter Fifteen

A meadowlark trilled, anticipating the morning's arrival. Part of Angelique wished it were a nightingale and that there was still the entire eve to come again. A warm arm slipped around her waist, a hand took hers tenderly.

"Sleep now, beloved." The words were a rich, low sound that encircled her heart as wholly as that simple embrace held her body. "I am here."

"I won't let you go," Angelique mumbled, snuggling more closely against her lover and settling, content once more.

Drew's soft laughter echoed in her ears as she drifted off. Angelique never remembered it sounding so genuine before. And holding that thought, she slept.

Angelique woke alone, but began to laugh as soon as she opened her eyes, a laughter that brought tears of joy to her eyes as she beheld her room.

It was covered with fair, pink roses. Her quilt was covered with the blossoms, the floor littered so thickly that the carpet was completely lost. Tucked into the hanging sheer draperies on her terrace doors, dusted across chairs, vanity and hearth, strewn about the entire room were thousands of blooms. Only the pillow beside her was nearly bare. It held but a single, thornless stem with two blooms and a pair of letters.

Angelique was touched to see those thorns had been snipped by hand, not by magic. She pushed her dark hair aside as she sat up and reached for the letters. One she set aside for a while; it was from her mother. But the other was unsealed, and she recognized the fine script as Drew's.

Angelique read:

I am not far, Beloved. The locket will bring me if you have need.

Forgive my absence. I'd promised to lend Culdun's kin help in clearing the feast. Since my magick created many of the fire and dancing rings, my magick is needed to banish them.

Shall I see you in our garden for tea? Or if not, I will seek you here in your chambers.
Drew

Tea? Angelique glanced at the mantel clock in stunned surprise. It was indeed late in the afternoon. Chagrin at the decadence melted into wry amusement as she stretched slowly. She luxuriated in the sweet ache of her body, remembering it was truly a testament to a decadent sort of night — a night of purely mortal magick and love.

Smiling, Angelique reached for her mother's letter.

Angelique was shaking as she bent over the fountain's edge. The words of the reflection spell lingered in the air. At the sound of footsteps, she turned. With a broken sob, Angelique held up the letter from Aloysius' household. "When did this arrive?"

"The caravan returned just before the fete last night," Drew replied, gently taking the paper from Angelique. She concentrated on the letter, reading the lingering signature of time on it. "It arrived yesterday."

"My mother is dying," Angelique cried. "What time is it in the outside world?" Angelique pressed anxiously. "How much time has passed already?"

"You could not find her with the water spell," Drew said, guiding Angelique back to the fountain.

"I couldn't concentrate well enough," Angelique admitted.

"I will find her for you." Drew's arms encircled Angelique from behind. "Stay very still and you will see what I see."

Drew spoke a few soft words and moved her hands, palms downward, over the water. The trickling of the fountain stopped. The glassy surface stilled and became mirrored silver. Smoke swirled in the glittering depths. Then images emerged in hazy, indistinct patterns, and slowly Angelique recognized her mother's room.

"This place is warded against my visions." Drew's confused murmur was nearly inaudible. "That is strange indeed."

"There is Mama," Angelique whispered.

"She lives. See the woman who is moving away to sit? She is the nurse."

"Yes. I see her. I see no death candles nor coins."

"No candles," Drew agreed, but the mists swirled too thickly to show coins if they had been laid to the woman's eyelids. "Let us try another room."

But the mists became thicker as they moved from room to darkened room.

"Is it night there, do you think?" Angelique breathed, praying that was the cause of such stillness.

"Yes," Drew replied.

The images shifted to another room, and Angelique recognized Aloysius' chamber. It had been so grandly decorated with Drew's own gifts that she barely recognized it.

"He should not have kept my things if he did not want me to reach him," Drew observed. "See how clearly they cast light for our seeing."

"But he is still barely visible."

"I should have sent him a four-poster and canopy." There was, however, no humor in the calm voice.

"Is there another with him?"

"Has he a mistress?" Drew asked.

The thought startled her. Wryly, Angelique remembered Aloysius' mistrust of women and his lust for gold. "Only his money, I would think." The mists grew blacker and it became difficult to discern anything in the dusky light. The picture shifted and they were outside of the house now. The moon glittered, nearly full. Clouds moved in pale blue streaks across the starry sky.

"See, it is night, not death."

It was reassuring to know that was true. Then it seemed as if a rain began. Muddy waters shimmered across wet cobblestones. Droplets fell. The scene rippled as if it were a reflection disturbed in a rain puddle and, gradually, the images melted away.

Angelique blinked. She glanced up as the pitter-patter of the rain continued. Surprised, she noted the fountain had begun again. She realized abruptly there was no rain after all.

Drew shifted, began to move away, but Angelique grasped Drew's hands and pulled them tight around her. It was then she felt the trembling in the tall form that leaned against her, almost needing her support.

"Are you all right?" Angelique prompted softly. She was afraid to turn around, least she set the other off balance. The head beside her own nodded wearily, and she kissed the soft cheek.

Drew straightened stiffly, blinking as if returning from a dream. Angelique did turn then, her hands rubbing warmth and strength back into those cold arms. A faintly derisive laugh met Angelique's worried gaze as Drew admitted, "It would have been easier to send someone to investigate than to stand here and search through those mists."

Relieved that Drew's dry humor had returned, Angelique smiled. "You couldn't know the place would be warded against you."

"Not all of it is," Drew amended. A dark frown furrowed her brow. "Just Aloysius and some of the rooms. Those things are hidden by some sort of talisman made specifically to hide certain images from me."

"That was the black smoke?"

"Yes."

Angelique shivered though the sun was warm.

"He cannot harm you here," Drew reminded her. The soft timbre of her voice chilled as she added, "I will never allow him to harm you again." Angelique nodded, her face against Drew's chest. She didn't speak for a long moment, prompting Drew to ask, "There is something more?"

Angelique pulled away a little. She looked up into Drew's face, her eyes pleading for understanding. "My mother is dying, Drew. My brothers write that she asks for me. I want to see her. I need to go back."

Drew collapsed as if she had been struck. Her face crumpled, her shoulders dipped and her hands fell; a bleakness more terrible than the haunted hollowness had ever been seemed to wash suddenly into her dark eyes.

"Drew!" Angelique sobbed as her fingers clenched at the other's sleeve. Drew pulled. "Please, Drew! Please try to understand. She's my mother! She's dying. I must see her. I can't let her die in that house — not in his house! I have to be there for her. I need to be there!"

Culdun appeared suddenly at the edge of the gardens, his expression puzzled. "You called, my Liege?"

"Angelique wishes to return home, Culdun. See to it at once."

The Old One rocked back as if struck.

"Only for a short while!" Angelique cried. "I will come back to you, Drew. You may ask anything of me but don't ask me not to do this. Don't make me choose! I love you! How many times must I say it? How many ways must I prove it? I'll do anything to stay with you! But please, Drew..." Her voice broke, faltering to a whisper. "I beg of you. Just see this for what it is. It is not a betrayal of you. Without her, I would not be here to love you at all—"

Something flickered across Drew's stricken face. "You would promise to return to me?"

"Yes!" Angelique cried. She stepped in front of Drew and took the other woman's hands, realizing that Drew had heard little of the truth, but had thought instead that Angelique meant to leave for good. She squeezed Drew's hands and, fastening her gaze onto the other's dark eyes said, "Feel me, Drew! I am your love. I belong to you. You cannot cast me aside so easily. We are bound by our hearts, our bodies, our spirits. If you remember nothing of last night, remember that at least."

Drew's eyes flashed as if she did not believe Angelique's

words. In a voice that rang with challenge, she said, "Then you will marry me."

Quietly, Angelique opened a hand and uttered her spell. The silver rose appeared on her palm. She offered Drew the token, her voice steady and firm. "I will marry you."

There was a pause, until Drew lifted the rose from Angelique's palm. She took a step away, turning the token over and over. When she turned back, she said, "You said I can ask anything of you?"

Angelique stiffened, but she nodded.

"I ask that you return in two weeks' time."

Angelique's stomach quivered at the brief span allotted. Death was not always a predictable occurrence.

"If you do not," the voice grew hushed, "my magick may not be able to reach you to bring you back at all."

"Remember, this valley shifts in time," Culdun said softly. He stood quite near her now, and he met her searching gaze evenly. "Because you are mortal and live here, we are somewhat bound to your time and birthplace. But when you are gone —" He shrugged solemnly. "We may wait two weeks. After that, we might not be able to fetch you even by an overland excursion."

"If all my studies of the stars and the powers are finally correct, there will be a new moon in two weeks." Drew straightened, turning again to face Angelique. "My magick will be at its strongest and our worlds will be one. Even if your father grows fearful and wards the entire county against my sorcery, I will still be able to open your way home."

Drew extended her hand. In the palm lay a brooch of ivory and pearl. Angelique gasped, recognizing the symbol of the intertwined snakes. The ivory made them into ghostly images of the Old Ones' designs.

"This is my talisman for your protection in the outside world. It carries the ancient strength of my friends' world and taps the powers of my own magick."

Drew came near and folded the talisman gently into Angelique's palm. "And it carries a piece of my soul as well."

Angelique lifted startled eyes to her lover's.

"Return and make me whole, Angelique."

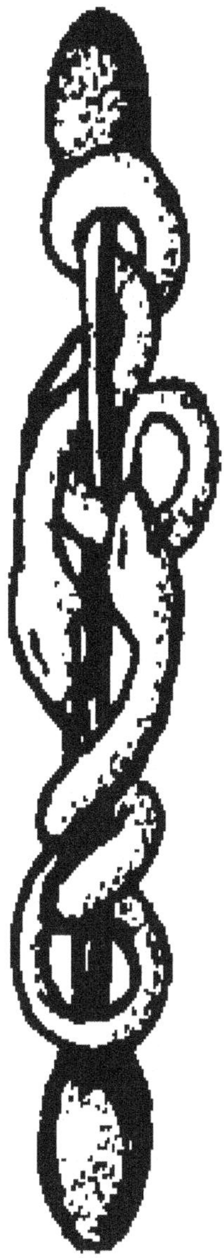

"But what if something should happen to it?" Angelique breathed in horror, unwilling to lose both the women she loved so dearly in this life.

"I am immortal, beloved."

"But that does not protect you from being hurt!" Angelique rasped.

"I will be fine. Once you return to me." Slender fingers silenced Angelique's unspoken protest. "Return and be mine."

"I am already yours, my Liege," she whispered, kissing Drew's fingertips. "I promise I will return."

"To marry me?"

"Yes. I will hold you to the marriage by your very own vow."

"By our vow, my Lady."

Chapter Sixteen

Culdun escorted Angelique down the winding cobblestone lane as far as the valley gates. She took horses laden with fine clothes and gifts. Aloysius and her brothers would expect as much of her now, she knew. But it was not a thing that made the going easier. Stepping through those gates into Drew's magick portal, and stepping out into Aloysius' court, had taken more courage than she had ever known she possessed.

The selfishness and delighted greed of her two brothers in response to the gifts had been oddly reassuring. But it was one of the few things she found unchanged. Ivan's polished manners she found especially disconcerting. The all-too-ready smile puzzled her as she thought the veneer was too thin to mask the cruel glint lurking behind his eyes. Angelique still remembered well the rough riding lessons he had given her as a youngster, and the numerous falls she had endured in the stone court.

However, the introduction of Ivan's new wife explained much of his surface changes. The woman, Marguerite, had been widowed twice, and each time she had taken over the management of the shops and trading contracts of her late husbands' businesses. Angelique had shivered at the meeting. Aloysius had not arranged this marriage; those two were too well matched. Greed for greed, plot for plot, the pair would probably rule the Continent's trade before the end of the decade.

Her younger brother, Phillip, she found she could only pity. His head-strong willfulness had become drunken pettiness in the brief year she'd been gone. She supposed there was little else she should have expected, between the sudden arrival of so much wealth and the taunting of his older brother. Marguerite's arrival couldn't have helped matters either, since she viewed his drunkenness as an impediment to his usefulness in forming another trading liaison through marriage.

Yet it was her mother's cheerful greeting that puzzled Angelique the most. Certainly she had grown a year older, but money had brought wood and good food which had, in turn, brought a faint bit of color back into her cheeks. The nurse and chambermaid were nearly as delighted as her mother to see the fine woman their charge was always talking of, and they were pleased to know the letters had been so well received.

When questioned about her mother's health, they merely seemed confused and admitted to a slight fever and a cough a few weeks back, but both assured Angelique that it had been nothing serious. Perhaps, they suggested, she'd been confusing news of her mother's health with Aloysius' failing condition.

Of Aloysius himself, she saw nothing at first. Ivan said he had taken to his bed with a cough last winter and had chosen never to arise again. Ivan admitted the man was not doing well, but he also suggested that Aloysius had merely grown more cantankerous. He would see his daughter when he felt like seeing her. Until then she would simply have to be patient.

When pressed for the reasons behind the alarming letter, Ivan shrugged and seemed to grow increasingly uncomfortable, until Marguerite stepped forward to accept the blame for summoning Angelique. After all, Marguerite said, she understood how fond of one another mother and daughter were. Marguerite also pointed out that the nurse and chambermaid had not been completely honest regarding the seriousness of the fever and she freely admitted that she'd told Ivan to ask Angelique to come for a visit.

The conflicting stories formed an uneasy knot in Angelique's stomach. Although the tale could easily be true, she did not feel that Marguerite was being completely honest with her. Angelique did not like this new household of Aloysius' any better than the old. It was merely a different household, but not any safer, especially with Aloysius ensconced in his bedchambers and Ivan's ruling by proxy.

"Come now, my dear Angelique," Marguerite smiled sweetly, pausing in her needlework to offer an almost compassionate glance, "surely you had guessed. And since you have seen him, could you not tell by mere sight?"

"Come now yourself, Madam." Phillip bowed with a leering, mocking grin as he rose from the parlor's window seat. "Surely you can't expect my dear sister to see so clearly. After all, the girl's been away for nearly a year. People change. How was she to know Father had not merely become a man of leisure?"

"For pity's sake, leave off!" Ivan snarled. He turned from the fire's hearth and added, "Angelique has no more love for the man than we. Have you forgotten the poor girl's beatings?"

Angelique managed not to flinch as Ivan's hand patted her shoulder. She mustn't underestimate him, she reminded herself as she wondered about this new brotherly concern and awkward affection. She also wondered if Marguerite knew of his terrible temper. Marguerite did not seem like a fool; most likely, she simply looked the other way when it reared its ugly head.

"And what — precisely — is he dying from?" Angelique persisted yet again in an attempt to get a direct answer.

"I don't know, dear," Marguerite said. "He was suffering from the cough before I joined the household. That was at Midwinter."

"It was just his winter cough," Ivan shrugged with a politely forced smile. "You remember, the same one that takes to him every year?"

Phillip snorted as he tried to laugh and drink at the same time. Wine sputtered down his vest.

"Yes, well," Ivan waved his hand dismissively, "obviously it wasn't just a winter's cough this time."

"And the old miser brought it on himself." Phillip dropped down on the bench beside his sister. With a smirk, he sprawled back against the mammoth oak table. "He wouldn't spend the money on the doctor."

"But why?" Angelique pressed, deliberately turning back to Ivan. "Didn't you say the doctor came weekly this winter to see Mama? Would it have been so much trouble to—"

"Ah, you speak so rationally." Ivan chuckled almost sadly. "He had something of a fever, Angelique. He wasn't quite himself. He started raging about nothing. But at first that didn't seem unusual. By the time we realized how ill he was, it was too late."

"Yet no one thought to tell me?"

"What?!" Phillip scoffed into his cup. "And have your precious Lord and Master cut us off without another word?"

"We have had quite enough of you, Phillip," Marguerite warned softly. With an insolent shrug the man rose and departed. Marguerite sighed, wearily setting her embroidery down. "You must forgive the oversight, Angelique. Ivan had not thought you cared much about Aloysius one way or the other, and Phillip," she smiled dryly, "he was preoccupied with your Betrothed's wealth."

Whereas you are not? Angelique mused, as she began to understand just how interested they really were.

"It is true though that once Papa is gone, Angelique's bride price will be gone as well." Ivan sat down on the corner of the table. His body language suggested he was addressing his wife, but he was uncomfortably close to Angelique and seemed suddenly to loom above her. "Perhaps we should begin to redistribute some of our holdings to compensate?"

"Our Venetian friends, perhaps?"

Uncomfortably Angelique rose and drifted nearer the hearth, half-listening. She was no merchant herself, but she knew the value of Drew's magicked goods. She was not fooled by this casual ploy and was not surprised when Ivan finally turned to her with the question she'd been awaiting.

"Of course, we may be doing the man an injustice. What would you say, Angelique?"

"I'm sorry, Ivan." She blinked, hoping to appear just a little lost. "I wasn't listening properly."

"Are we doing your gentlemen a disservice? Assuming he's not interested in further business with us?"

"My Liege?" Angelique shrugged faintly. "I don't know. I've never much been part of — trading contracts and such."

"Come, come," Ivan teased her none too lightly. "Since when has docile meekness ever suited you, sister?"

She put an icy chill into her voice, her chin lifting as she chose a reason he would value. "Can you imagine, brother, the difference between a riding crop and a sorcerer's hand?"

Ivan's eyes darkened. But he said no more.

"Angelique, my dear," Marguerite interjected smoothly. "Are you saying you're unhappy with this magickian?"

"No." Angelique stared into the fire's leaping flames again, remembering Drew's arms encircling her that night in the faery's mist. She wished her guardian was nearer.

"Because if you are, there are ways around—"

"I'm fine, Marguerite." Angelique forced a smile through her tiredness. "Honestly. I'm merely saying that life with my Liege is different than it was for me here." She glanced at her brother. "Is it any wonder I'd change a bit, Ivan?"

He didn't appear to wholly trust her argument. But with a wary smile he agreed to let the matter go.

"That is a lovely brooch you're wearing." Marguerite had resumed her needlework again and barely seemed to glance at the pin. "Is it a favorite? You seem to wear it often."

"Yes." Angelique felt her throat close. She felt suddenly like a mouse caught between two very hungry cats.

"It's an unusual design. I keep thinking I've seen it some place before?"

"I wouldn't know," Angelique replied. "If you'll both excuse me, it's been a long day."

She left them, her stomach a knot of tension. She had four days left to her visit, although they were unaware of her plans to leave them so soon. Four days in which they would persistently seek a way to bind Drew to their schemes while Angelique would desperately search for a way to protect her mother. She had not a doubt that the extra servants and care would vanish with Aloysius' death. For although he had always cared what the townsfolk thought of his family image, Ivan held little respect for others' opinions, and even less for his mother. With Marguerite's help, Angelique was sure that Ivan would soon come to see that Mama was a costly expenditure that should be disposed of quickly and quietly.

One solution seemed obvious: she could offer to extend Drew's trade agreement in exchange for a continuation of care. But she was loath to bind her beloved to such awful creatures and wondered if there might be another solution. Angelique fell asleep wondering if the temperament of Drew's stepmother had been something akin to Marguerite's.

"There is something wrong, Culdun. I tell you I *feel* it!" Drew's hands closed into fists. "If only I could see her. But that damnable man even has his sons warded against me now!"

Culdun said nothing as he watched Drew pace before the hearth. There was nothing to say. They could only wait.

The four days passed far too quickly. Chaos descended like a violent storm that very night, leaving a terrible destruction in its wake. Aloysius' intermittent bellowing ceased quite abruptly. His fever rose. In two days, he was dead.

Then Angelique's mother became terribly and suddenly ill. With the household staff in turmoil over the death duties and Ivan's gracious hosting of the-not-so-mournful town merchants, Angelique discarded her satin skirts and petticoats to don simpler garb to help nurse her mother through the strange seizures. She did not think her mother was as grief-stricken as Marguerite surmised; Aloysius was no real loss to her. But what worried Angelique more was the danger of the woman's fragile bones being shattered by these violent shakes.

As unexpectedly as it had begun, the illness ended. Marguerite seemed smugly satisfied. The doctor shrugged, shook his head and left. Phillip sneered and praised his sister on so adroitly avoiding the late afternoon funeral. With that comment the last of Angelique's patience fled. Pushing past her brother, she retreated into her room, sank down on the bed and took her head in her hands.

Tonight, finally, was the new moon. Tonight she would go home. She would ask Drew to continue working with these

The Wait

folk for Mama's sake. She trusted that Drew would find some way to deal with these despicable people she found herself related to. She no longer had the patience for them.

Tonight, beneath a starlit sky, her betrothed would open the gates for her again. It would not matter how many warded pieces Ivan hung about the walls; it would not matter what pretty stories he told about those odd, little relics. He need never be the wiser.

Angelique turned to search for the blue velvet and gold-threaded dress she knew Drew loved, the gown that reminded Angelique of moonless nights and star-bright skies. Every time she wore it, upon seeing her for the first time, Drew would stop and stare, wide-eyed as if she could not believe such a beautiful woman might ever grace her presence. She would wear it tonight. In celebration.

The parlor was dark. The embers in the hearth barely glowed. Drew sat alone and unmoving, engulfed by the shadowy depths of the chair. In her hand, she held the silver rose. Her thoughts were in turmoil and, without thinking, she closed her fist about the delicate flower, not feeling the thorns slice into her skin.

Blood dripped in lacy patterns down her hand like dark and dangerous tears.

"Phillip, have you seen my brooch?"

He snickered and walked past her on up the stairs. And now Angelique knew to fear the worst. Angelique cursed herself. She should have been paying more attention and remembered to re-pin the brooch to her other garments.

"My goodness, Angelique. You're quite pale!" Marguerite remarked. Her tapestry frame had been pushed aside, but she did not rise from the small couch.

"What's wrong, Angelique?" Ivan stepped forward with a frown. "You haven't caught Mother's stomach ailment, have you?"

Phillip's laughter called their little bluff as he bounded down the steps. He tossed a heavy key across to his brother and rebuked them both. "She's finally noticed, you fools. Did you think she had no brains at all?"

"Phillip, please." Marguerite sounded faintly bored. She waved her hand toward the cupboard where the spirits were kept. "Amuse yourself and let us tend to the poor woman."

"My brooch," Angelique pressed, "the one with the two snakes. Where is it?"

"Oh that, my dear." Marguerite settled back, seemingly less disturbed as she returned to her tapestry work. "Ivan has it. A servant found it lying about somewhere. Seems the clasp was broken."

"I thought I'd have it mended for you." Her older brother smiled sweetly as he pulled the piece from his vest pocket.

He made no move to return it, however, and Angelique barely stopped herself from bounding forward to grab it. Something about his stance reminded her all too well of those taunting 'get-it-if-you-can' games of their childhood.

"I did, however, tell Ivan to speak to you about it first." Angelique glanced back at Marguerite. The woman appeared oblivious to the growing tension between them. "I reminded Ivan of your gentleman's penchant for magick and of the fact that this piece might not be mended by a mere jeweler's skill." Something in the blandness of the matron's voice made Angelique's stomach clench. "It was then that I remembered where I'd seen the piece before."

Angelique wet her lips and eyed Ivan nervously. He backed away toward the fire's hearth. Her throat felt dry, but she managed to ask, "And where was that, Marguerite?"

"With your Liege's caravans of goods, of course. One of those odd, little men always wore it pinned to a cloak or vest somewhere. Then I felt sure it was magicked."

"We rather thought," Ivan leaned against the mantle, examining the brooch with forced casualness, "this might be the piece which lets you all travel back and forth from that wicked palace to here."

Angelique looked to each of them anxiously, waiting.

"Yes," Ivan smiled, more sincerely this time, as his voice dropped. "Marguerite suggested we offer you safe haven from this monster that you so dislike."

"Monster?" Angelique blinked. "I've never said anything about my Liege being a monster."

"Oh, come," Marguerite tisk-tisked the young woman. "It has been nearly a year and you've avoided marrying the man." The older woman's eyes narrowed shrewdly. "It's obvious you care nothing for him, which admittedly may not be all that unusual. As you said yourself, a sorcerer's hand can be a far worse fate than a mere leather strap."

"We thought," Ivan added, "you could stay here and we'll do our best to find you a more suitable husband. What about it now?"

"With a suitable bride price, I presume?" Angelique questioned bitterly. Behind her Phillip chortled in malicious delight.

"It would be unreasonable to expect you to marry a poor man, wouldn't it?" Ivan prompted. "And the sorcerer's marriage was conditional on your own agreement. I remember that quite specifically."

"Or your willingness to return me?" Angelique baited coyly.

"Ha! She sees right through your scheming plots, brother!" Phillip lifted his cup high in a toast. He rose and sauntered over, whispering to Angelique in an overly loud voice, "You're worth next to nothing to them if you return to your magickian's little palace. But should they sell you again? Well!"

"And if there was a way to return me and insure that more wealth would be forthcoming?" She queried to Marguerite in particular. "Would that not be an even better solution?"

"Go on," Ivan prodded warily.

"Have you forgotten Mama?"

The elder brother grunted.

"I am well aware that I am the daughter of the house,"

Angelique continued to address the matron. "It should have become my responsibility to tend Mama in her later years. There is compensation due my brother, I think."

"And you believe your sweet husband-to-be would agree?" Ivan sneered.

"My Liege would agree. I am denied nothing I ask for."

"But why this small thing? You know as well as I that it's an oft-ignored custom, even in the best of families, like ours."

"Our valley is isolated," Angelique returned rationally, though she did not feel calm inside. "The customs of outsiders are not well known. My Liege would not challenge my request on those grounds alone."

Marguerite stirred. "Ivan said your father-in-law is a Count. Is that true?"

The question startled her. Angelique nodded warily. "He was. He is dead now."

"Is the valley truly so isolated?"

"Yes."

"Your gentleman's king must be lax-handed with his taxes that your Liege has so much wealth. Or is the monarch so far away that his tithes are merely forgotten?"

"My Liege answers to no one, Madam. Land and folk need be loyal to only one — our own guardian."

"Your sorcerer?"

"My Liege."

With a faint shrug Marguerite addressed Ivan. "We had hoped to bind a new contract with the man, but it seems she's worthless to him. He's too powerful to waste so much coin on such an expensive whim as this little trollop."

"You dare—" Angelique began, but Marguerite talked over her words and continued.

"Custom or none, the sorcerer would not allow himself to be so abused. And we have nothing else that might even vaguely amuse him."

"But we do have Angelique," Phillip grinned. He was enjoying his sister's shocked and angry flush.

"Here, yes," Marguerite admitted. "The house and shop are warded against the man —"

"Expensive safeguards," Ivan grumbled. "You're certain Florence's trade will be as rich?"

"Nothing will ever be as rich as what you have now!" Angelique's temper flared. Ivan spun, ready to strike.

"She speaks the truth," Marguerite allowed placidly, her tone halting Ivan.

Brother and sister were standing very close together. The brooch was inches away from Angelique's fingertips. At the same moment, they both realized this. Ivan's eyes grew wide. Angelique leapt for the brooch as Marguerite's voice shouted, "Break it quickly, Ivan. Toss it in the fire!"

"No!"

Ivan danced out of Angelique's reach, his fingers snapping the brooch in two, and the hearth flames exploded in a wild whoosh of flame as the pieces were swallowed. Colors of bright green and blue danced in swirling, twisting vines. The man laughed in triumph, backing away from the inferno to watch the smoking tendrils of snakes writhe and lift and then vanish in yellow flames.

"No!" Angelique dove toward the hearth, even though she knew it was too late.

Ivan kicked her to her knees, then kicked her again for good measure.

"Phillip, help your brother," Marguerite called brusquely.

The man gulped the last of his wine and stood uncertainly. But even drunk, he and Ivan could easily subdue Angelique. They dragged her along the flagstone floor and away from the hearth.

"You can't do this!"

"I'm afraid we most certainly can," Marguerite smiled.

Angelique felt her heart grow cold. The malicious pleasure was too bright in the matron's eyes.

"It's a shame he hasn't married you. I admit when we invited you to visit, we had not expected to find you unwed. As his wife, you might just have been able to negotiate a contract for your mother's care. But this other venture will do just as nicely."

"My Liege will come for me," she shouted.

"Your sorcerer will find you... eventually," Marguerite

soothed, still smiling. "But only after you've been moved from this house. Until then?" She ended with a delicate shrug.

"*No!*" Angelique hissed, rage flaring her new powers to life. Her voice rose as she cried, "You hide from sight, but my Liege knows where I am. The moon is new and the power bright! *The Door will open!*"

A crack of thunder shook the hearth behind Ivan. He and Phillip both jumped away from Angelique for a moment, looking to Marguerite for reassurance. Smoke billowed and there was a sound like a banshee's wail that split the air like lightning. Marguerite merely looked annoyed. "Enough!" she bellowed. As smoke cleared, she nodded at Ivan. He grabbed Angelique's arms again. "It was nothing. The spell in the brooch is properly broken. The thunder marked it, as she knew it would. Now, Phillip, you brought the key. Use it."

Culdun came racing along the corridor even as his Liege was striding near.

"The gateway! I was at the valley's gate waiting!" The Old One abruptly reversed his direction as the grim figure marched by. "My Liege! The gate opened. She tried. For a brief moment, it did open!"

"I know." The voice was stony. The woman flung out her hand and the terrace doors swept open as if blown by a mighty wind. "Something is wrong, Culdun. And it is time to see what."

Chapter Seventeen

"No!" Angelique's fists beat the wood, pummeling uselessly as the laughter beyond the door faded. When Angelique understood there would not be a reprieve, she sobbed, sliding to the floor. It couldn't end this way! It must not! When her tears were done, she steeled her nerves and began to look for a solution.

The window was shuttered. An old mirror lay nearby. Slowly, her eyes adjusted. She was in the very small room beneath the turret's eves. It was flanked by Marguerite's room and the private stairwell. Thick plaster walls and strong timbers would muffle her cries. In here, neither the servants nor her mother would ever hear her.

It was ironic that she now found herself in the same room she had used as a child to hide from Aloysius. She'd never known there was a key. And now there were wards as well. Without the brooch, she was not certain Drew could even send someone to search for her. But would she? Which assumption would she follow — that Angelique was in trouble and needed her aid or that Angelique had abandoned her? Angelique hoped it would be the former, but feared the latter.

Her fingers fluttered uselessly about her clothing. What could she do? The talisman had been broken. Drew might even think she'd broken it herself! No. She could not bear the thought of that. As her fingers pulled her hair away from her collar, they brushed something else. The locket! She had almost forgotten it completely. Encircling it with her fingers, she closed her eyes and called to Drew as loudly as she could, with her voice and with her heart, all the while hoping the magick would be able to penetrate through the wards and across the distance and reach her beloved.

The image of Aloysius' house shimmered and dissolved in the fountain pool. Drew cursed, turning to Culdun with barely controlled rage, and spat, "She calls! From beyond my boundaries she calls in need and I stand here shackled!"

"My Liege, what about the brooch? Is not the brooch yours?"

"She no longer has it! And it will take a year to make another!" Drew paced, looking like a caged animal.

"But, my Liege, the brooch *belongs* to you."

A harsh breath hissed through Drew's teeth. Her eyes stared off into night. Slowly, as if feeling the way around the edges of a room in the dark, Drew took a step forward and then another.

"*My* talisman," she breathed, halting again. "All beneath my protection —"

"—belong to you," Culdun finished, adding, "And treasures stolen are retrievable. If you seek the brooch, will you not find her near?"

"Before she left us, what did Angelique say?!"

"That she loved you. That she would return."

"And that *she was mine!* In open court of this magicked land — you witnessed it yourself."

Understanding lit Culdun's face. "Yes, my Liege, she did!"

"Then let those wretched wards blind my distant sight. With stallion and sword I'll fetch her myself!"

Thunder shook the windowpanes though there was no storm near. Lightning clashed and black clouds rolled in to eclipse the starry sky. A stallion's shriek turned Phillip's head to the window. He dropped his cup as the lightning cracked again and he saw the white steed pawing the air. Opening his mouth to speak, he found he had no words to describe the black-garbed rider whose cape flowed behind like a river of blood. Lightning flashed a third time and illuminated a naked blade. Phillip stumbled back from the window.

"Have you the charms about you?" Marguerite asked blandly, not pausing in the careful counting of her stitches.

Ivan chuckled nastily and lifted his stein of ale from the mantelpiece.

The crash that splintered the door made even Marguerite look up. Wind gusted into the room, overturning chairs. Marguerite's tapestry frame lifted and she cried out once as it struck her in the head, then she collapsed to the floor, motionless. Ivan started toward her. Phillip fled toward the shadows near the staircase.

Drew extended one black-gloved hand, fingers spread, and Ivan was thrown backward. He cowered.

The wind died. The fire crackled wickedly. Silence descended.

Drew advanced, pinning Ivan against the wall with the tip of her broadsword inches from his chest. Ivan lifted his hands in supplication. "I have come for what is mine." Her voice left no room for argument.

Ivan forced a smile, lowering his hands to wipe palms cautiously along his thighs. "My Liege, what am I to say? Angelique feared you too much to confront you. She begged sanctuary from us."

Drew did not respond. Ivan licked his lips. There was a long tense silence. Suddenly, he leapt to the side and away, hands scrabbling for the sword hanging over the fire. Drew whirled and, seeing his objective, uncoiled like a snake. Before he could reach it, Drew had sent the sword spinning out of reach.

She brought the broadsword down on the table he'd tried to put between them, splitting it neatly in two.

Phillip screamed.

Ivan was now pinned between Drew and the hearth. She raised the broadsword again and leveled it at his chest. "If you try anything so foolish again, I will gut you like the pig you are. Now, where is she?"

"Don't tell, Ivan. She's all we have!" Phillip whined from the shadows near the staircase.

Without turning from Ivan, Drew extended her hand. Black-gloved fingers, long and menacingly mean, pinched the air as if squashing a bug. Phillip screamed again as ceramic plates, crystal vases and a variety of other earthenware shattered all around him. Something against Ivan's chest popped with a sickening sound and he scrabbled in his clothing, his fingers coming back empty. Drew had crushed Marguerite's talisman where it had hung about his neck.

"Now give me what is mine or I will begin to pull you limb from limb... and you can imagine which member I'll begin with."

Ivan looked stricken. Drew turned to Phillip. "Bring her!"

"The — the key!" Phillip pointed frantically to his brother. "He has the key!"

Ivan had just begun to pull it from his vest when it vanished.

"And now you have it," Drew's faceless voice corrected Phillip. "Fetch her. *Now!*"

The younger man scrambled up the stairs on all fours.

Marguerite groaned. Ivan looked to Drew; she shook her head, but backed up a little so that she could keep them both in sight. Upstairs, a door crashed open and footsteps rushed overhead. A moment later, Angelique all but flew down the stairs.

"Drew!"

Drew shifted the sword to her right hand and extended the left. Angelique melted against her. Without taking her eyes from the others, Drew asked, "Are you all right? Have they hurt you?"

"No. I'm fine. You came — you could come?" Angelique laughed brokenly, fingers running along the edges of the crimson cowl. Angelique lifted her hands toward the cowl and paused, asking permission. Drew nodded once. Angelique pushed the cloak away and beamed into Drew's familiar face.

Phillip, who had crept down the stairs after Angelique, let loose a shocked cry. Ivan shouted, "No! It can't be. You're her Liege? *You?*" But Angelique only smiled and kissed Drew boldly on the mouth.

Marguerite groaned and sat up. Drew looked to the woman and started. Angelique felt a tremor run through Drew's body.

"What is it?" Angelique asked.

But Drew just stared.

Marguerite turned her face fully toward the couple and smiled slowly. Taking her time, she brushed her hair from her face and dabbed at the cut the tapestry frame had made on her forehead. "Ah, Drew," she breathed. "We meet again at last."

Angelique looked from one to the other, confused. Then, slowly, realization dawned.

Marguerite rose, a bit unsteadily at first, then more confidently. "Did you think I could forget you? You and all your sins? Did you think I would actually let you achieve some sort of a normal life? Experience love? That after all this time I wouldn't be watching?" She laughed. It ended in a shriek that sent Phillip running up the stairs again.

Ivan cocked his head at her. She looked at him. "Ivan, dear boy. Don't think I don't love you. You are... sweet. But you were just a useful pawn in a much, much larger game."

He colored dangerously and took a step towards her. "What —"

Marguerite cut him off with a wave of her hand and he slumped down, unconscious. She turned back to Drew.

Drew faced to Angelique and said quietly, "You stand aside. I don't want you hurt."

"How very touching," Marguerite remarked. "When I found you were still living it was an unexpected surprise. When I heard you'd taken a... concubine, I decided to come and have a look for myself. How convenient that Ivan just happened to need a wife, one with some knowledge of," she paused and spat, "business."

Her grin grew wicked. "So, Drew, has your heart grown cold and bitter during your many years of imprisonment? Haven't those vile passions of youth tainted all your ambitions? Surely you're not still confined to simply controlling one insignificant wench at a time? How much time have you given over to planning your revenge? Against me? Against my daughter, the very one you thought loved you, as if such an act were possible? Love *you?*" She laughed again as though she found this thought too comic for words.

"Drew," Angelique's voice pierced the cackling laughter. "Don't listen to her."

Drew stood as if caught in a dream. She had cocked her head a little to one side and was looking at Marguerite with a strange half-smile on her face.

"I love you, Drew." Angelique cried. "From the moment we met. And I have pledged myself *willingly* to you. Please, Drew, don't listen."

Marguerite looked at Angelique as if seeing her for the first time. "Pledged yourself willingly? To a magickian? To a woman? Don't be a fool, child. There is no such thing as free will in the company of such a monster."

"You lie!" Angelique shrieked.

"Why would I lie, child? I have nothing to gain."

"Nothing to gain but my eternal imprisonment," Drew said suddenly. "And isn't that what you wanted all along? Or was I just a convenient means to an end? You wanted my father's wealth and you knew I found your daughter beautiful. I was an easy puppet to play, wasn't I? So young and naive, having grown up in a country where nothing was denied me, yet nothing truly given me either."

Drew took a step toward Marguerite and then another. When they were almost face to face, Drew said, "It's funny, but I thought you were... taller. You seemed much more menacing to me when I was hardly more than a child. But now, you are a foolish old woman, still playing at childish games. You have no power over me any longer, Marguerite."

The woman laughed. "Oh, but I do." She lifted her hand and a whirlwind erupted in the middle of the room, sending chairs, broken crockery and half-burned candles whipping through the air. Angelique cried out and took refuge behind an overturned table, peeking out to keep her beloved in sight.

Drew had not moved, but stood in the center of the maelstrom, blood-red cloak unfurled like a flag. For a long time, the wind shrieked in the house and Marguerite laughed. Angelique, understanding for the first time how terrible Marguerite must have seemed to a younger Drew felt her own rage bubbling up inside her. She poured her love out into Drew, opened her heart so that her own beloved could feel it washing over her like summer sunshine and springtime rain. And for a moment, the wind seemed to pause.

Drew turned her head a little and Angelique could see the beginning of a smile cross those fine lips. Then Drew bent her attention to the woman standing across from her. She lifted her hand toward Marguerite and the woman lifted from the floor.

Shrieking in indignant surprise, Marguerite struggled, but Drew closed her hand into a fist and the struggling stopped.

"You made one fatal mistake," Drew said, her voice lifting above the renewed rise of wind. "You never anticipated that someone would love me, would give herself to me and embrace the whole of who I am. And because Angelique has done just that, your curse has been nullified. It's over Marguerite. And I have won."

The woman glared, but Drew held her tightly. Lightening flashed and thunder boomed in the room. Still Drew did not falter. She lifted her other hand and shouted something into the rising storm.

Still held aloft, Marguerite began to age and wither; all the years that had passed since their last meeting suddenly caught up with the witch as Drew pealed away the woman's spell of longevity. In moments, Marguerite had become nothing more than dust that fell to the floor amid the broken crockery and fire's ash, and at last the magick winds faltered and died.

For a long moment, there was a terrible quiet in the room. Slowly, Drew turned toward Angelique and extended her hand. The young woman rose from her hiding place and came into her lover's arms.

"What did you do?" Angelique asked.

"I took away her powers," Drew said gently. "She was hundreds of years old. Once mortal again...."

Angelique shivered. She looked at her brother, Ivan, crumpled like a doll in the corner. "What of him?"

Drew shrugged. "Would you like me to turn him into a toad?"

Angelique laughed. "Can you really?"

Drew winked.

"No. I think it would be better to leave him. We never have to see them again, do we?"

"No. You never have to come here again, beloved," Drew replied.

"But," Angelique began. Her eyes went to the staircase and her mother's rooms beyond.

"I think there is a solution to that problem as well," Drew said.

Upstairs, Angelique knelt at her mother's bedside, Drew close behind her, while the nurse stood wide-eyed to one side.

"I fear they poisoned her the other day to distract me from Aloysius' death and to give them a chance to steal the brooch."

Drew stepped to the side of the bed. Lifting one hand, she let it move over the woman's frail body several inches above the quiet form. After a moment, Drew said, "She has been ill. And you were right. It was from a mild sort of poison. But she is safely through it now."

"And if they should try again?" Angelique breathed.

"You worry so much, my child," her mother whispered, coming fully awake. "Why should I want to live forever?"

"Mama, this is Drew."

Drew knelt beside the bed as the woman said, "At last. My daughter's fine magickian."

Drew offered a hesitant smile. "I hope you approve."

"I do." The old woman's eyes fluttered as if they might close.

"Madam?" Cautiously, Drew took the woman's hand in hers. "I have something to ask of you."

"If I can grant your wish, I will," the old woman allowed, eyes coming open again.

"You are not safe here. And I know it would make Angelique very happy if you would agree to come and live with us."

"Ah, the palace of wonders and strong wishing spells."

"The very same. There is a way for you to make the journey."

"A magickal way?"

Drew smiled. "A very magickal way. You have only to pledge yourself to me and it can be so."

A faint laugh, then, "I willingly pledge myself to one so gentle," she answered, her voice soft with sincerity.

To Angelique, Drew said, "You are witness to this oath." Angelique nodded. After a pause, Drew straightened and called, "Culdun."

The nurse fainted with a sharp cry and a thump as the Old One stepped into the room from nowhere. He noted her with a sigh. "My Liege?"

"Angelique's mother is to return with us."

Culdun smiled and shook his head at Angelique's worried expression. "I've seen the ailment before, Mistress. I won't break her." Angelique nodded. Gingerly, he picked up the woman and stepped through the magickal portal again.

They made their way back downstairs. At the hearth, Drew bent and retrieved something from the ashes. "This belongs to me, I think." She held up the two bits of the ivory broach. A few words later and it was whole again and unblemished.

Angelique let out a breath in relief. "I'd thought for certain they had destroyed it."

"It takes a great deal more than a mortal's hand and witch's fire to destroy a bit of a not-so-mortal soul, my love."

Drew reached for Angelique's hand again and they crossed the threshold together. The stallion neighed, head tossing and hoof pawing the cobblestones. Somewhere, a meadowlark began to sing. "Dawn is breaking," Angelique observed and shivered once.

"There is time enough." Drew sheathed her sword, mounted and lifted Angelique up before her. "Do you imagine my powers are solely limited by the mere cycling of night and day, beloved?"

Drew kissed Angelique gently. As they drew apart,

Angelique stroked the soft curve of her lover's cheek, but said nothing. There was nothing left to say.

Drew pulled her heels into the stallion's sides. With a leap, he lunged through the shimmering portal.

The meadowlarks trilled. In the east, the sun crested over the distant roofs and broke apart in glorious shafts of molten gold to touch the fields beyond. And far away, another sun rose upon two lovers, safe now and forever in their own timeless haven.

Gallery
Artwork by Skye Montague

Skye Montague is an author, artist and exotic dancer. She is an avid LGBT rights activist and a sex educator who specializes in consent and kink. Skye writes for Mariel Cove, a weekly erotic serial for queer women readers and several other series by Angels of Anarchy. Skye is also the primary artist for the Wolfe Campaign, creating many of the covers and interior artwork entirely as an volunteer. These ten interior artplates were inspired by the romance, truth and magick of *Roses and Thorns*. See more of Skye's artwork in Chris Anne's Talismans & Temptations: Aggar & Beyond, Shadows of Aggar, and Fires of Aggar. Discover Skye's writing by visiting:

http://marielcove.angelsofanarchy.com

Drew's Books

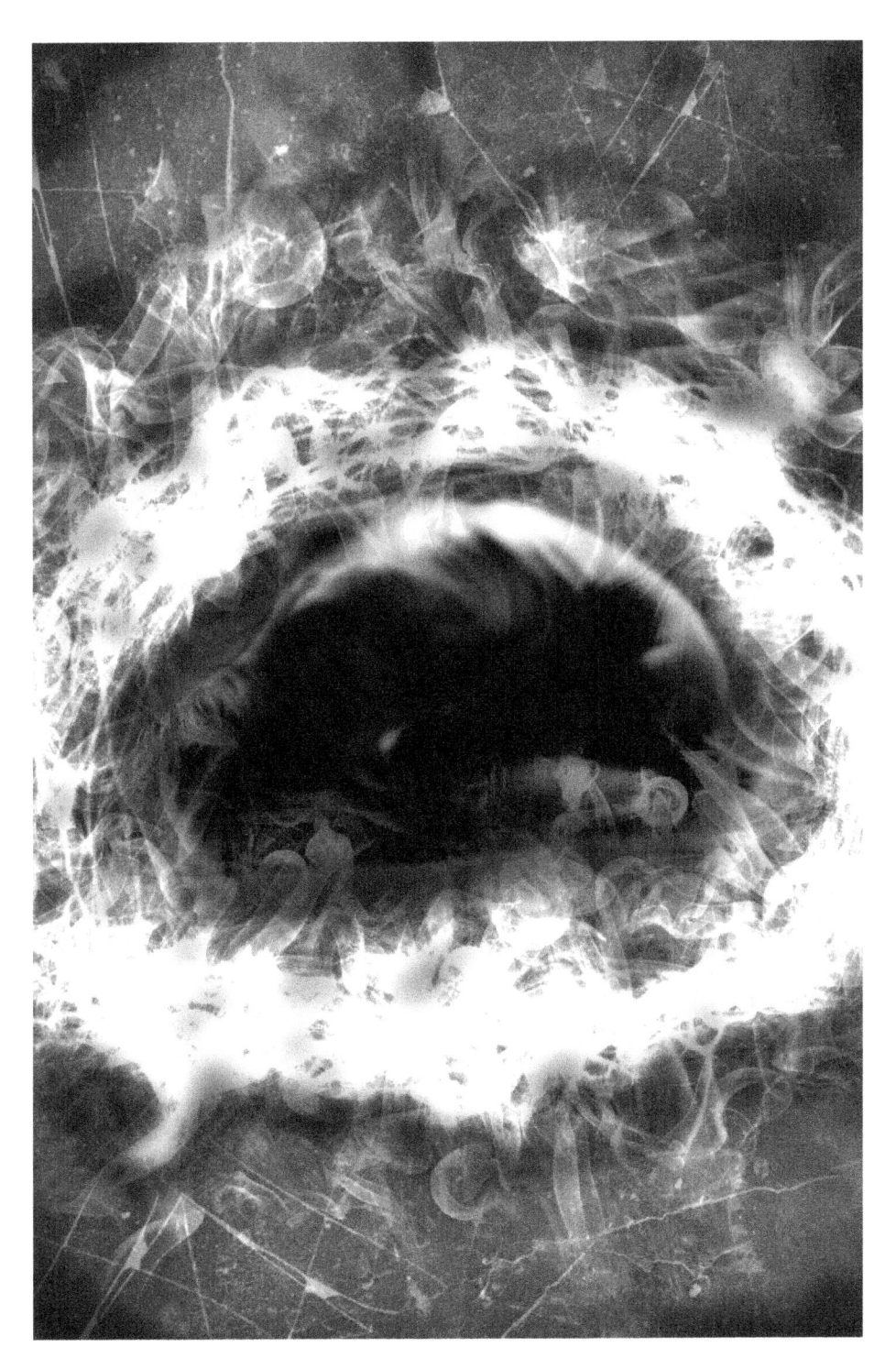

The Curse

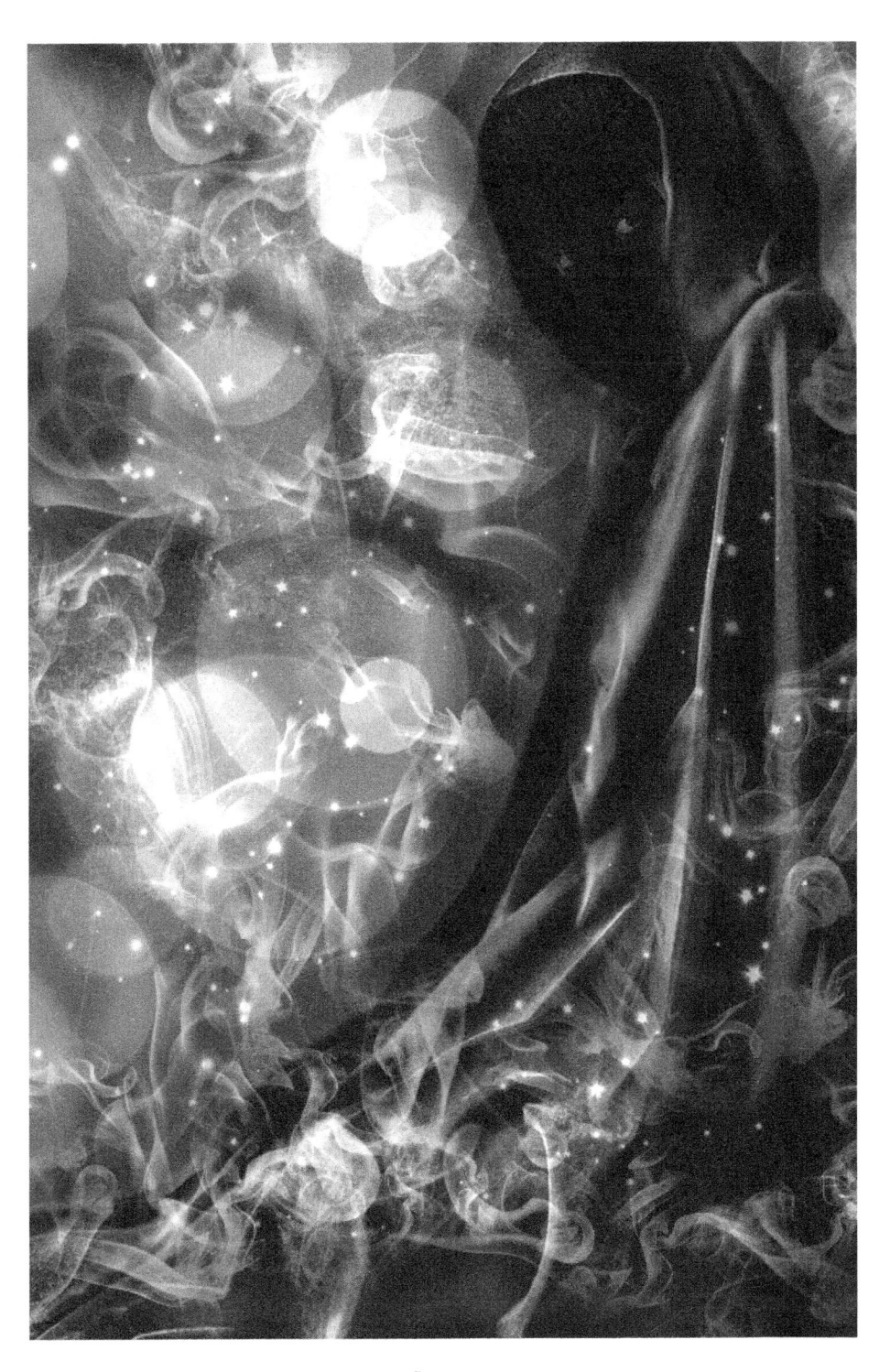

Drew

Fey

Meadow

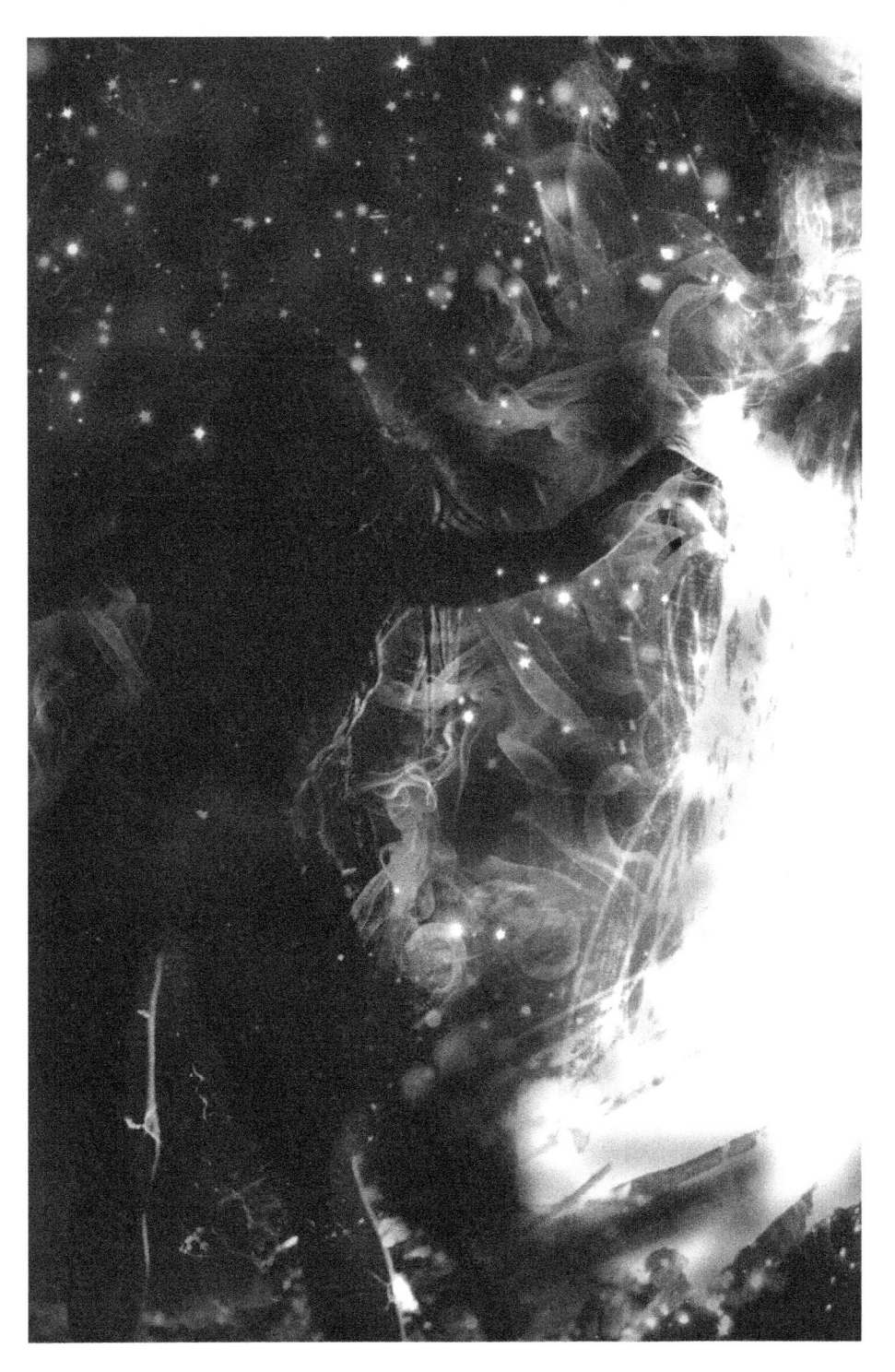

Fire Dance

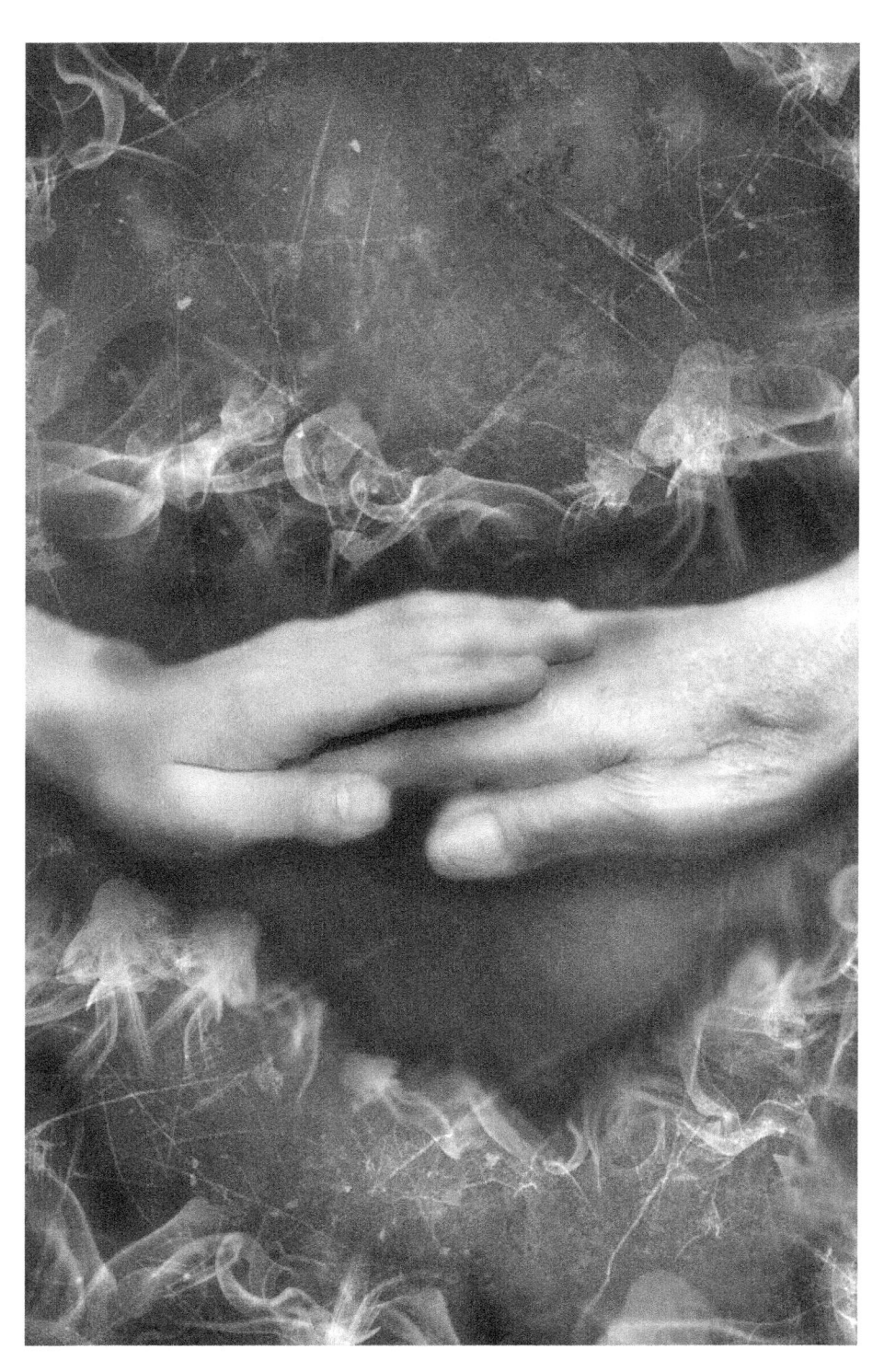

Hands Touch

Kiss

The Locket

The Rose

CPSIA information can be obtained at www.ICGtesting.com
Printed in the USA
LVOW04s2006060215

426021LV00033B/2668/P